The
Crash Team

Lawrence Helliwell

Dedication

Medicine can be a bitter sweet choice of career. One day, a giddy flight of head rushing highs, followed suddenly by unexpected turbulence and the occasional gut- wrenching nosedive. Most of us who have worked within the speciality for long enough have experienced a mix of these journeys, some which make us feel proud, and others which overwhelm us with remorse and regret at the things that we missed or got wrong.

This book has been written in tribute to the many amazing characters that I have met along the way in my own career. I assure you that the characters and scenarios are all purely fictional, but I do hope that I have managed to capture and convey some of the colour, camaraderie and mischief to share with you: the politics, the close shaves and the raw fun, as well as the origin of some of the shadows that follow many of us around still.

To those we harmed unintentionally along the way, through ignorance or arrogance, we cannot turn the clock back but are truly sorry. You stay in our memories forever and this book is dedicated to you.

To Tom, Marianne, Peter and Stewart
for providing the inspiration.

CHAPTER ONE: JUDGEMENT DAY

The three men sat miserably in the waiting area of the ornate building, filled with leather chairs, oak panels, and expensive carpets. A heady concoction of power and prestige.

Portraits of the great and the good adorned the walls, mostly with double-barrelled names, followed by a list of abbreviations to quantify their qualifications and self-worth. Eminent doctors. Mainly men, who had managed to transcend to the top of the medical ladder. Some said so that they could control their inferiors without demeaning themselves into making actual patient contact. They were in the very highest medical court in the land - The Medical Council's office in central London. Originally built in 1826 and now maintained by a combination of Government subsidies and compulsory fees for all doctors.

The deathly silence was broken by a Northern voice. "Well, I bet they know how to piss our subs down the drain," remarked the man to no one in particular. "Ironic," he added.

"Now we pay our own executioners, where once just a simple, small tip could ensure the head came off with one clean blow." He made a brief swishing moment with his hand, followed by a snort of derision.

He was a pleasant-faced fellow, with a bright gleam in his blue eyes and very shortly cropped hair, making his age difficult to estimate. Middle-age spread was clambering around his waist, but his clothing was surprisingly relaxed for the occasion, and athletic legs protruded from his three-quarter length shorts. He had munched through two chocolate bars and a bag of crisps already, whilst regularly glancing at the receptionist behind the desk, who hadn't failed to notice his attention or attempts at making eye contact. She continued to ignore him as best she could. He looked relaxed. Odd, considering the occasion. He wasn't.

His name was Dr David Ravensberg, an anaesthetist from the North West of England, who had found some brief infamy in the media. Better known as 'Dave the Rave' to those who knew him well, he was a man who managed to combine a cheeky wit with a sharp medical brain, despite its deficits in other areas of the white matter, especially the frontal lobe. Impossible to dislike. Unless he had slept with your wife or girlfriend, but fortunately, most of those affected were either blissfully unaware or had already forgiven him. There was just something about him that made you smile. He was a charmer. A few centuries ago, he would have been either a Lord or in prison. Or both. Nowadays, he would only be a Lord.

A few seats down sat Sid. His real name was much longer, but he was too polite to expect his colleagues to remember this. A GP from Leeds, born and trained in Patna, India. He was visibly nervous, quietly spoken and sat in a plain brown suit that had clearly seen happier times. An untouched sandwich sat by his side and seemed to sneer at him through its curling edges.

He was slight in build and slightly greying, but he hid this with ineptly applied dark hair dye. He was clutching something in his left hand as if his life depended upon it, whilst a grey sweat trickled down his forehead, despite the icy blast from the air conditioning. He was the very picture of abject misery. Every now and then, he would glance at his mobile phone, which had a deep crack down the screen where his son had dropped it whilst surfing the internet on his bicycle. His glasses had a bend in the middle, creating the semblance of facial asymmetry and a slight squint, but behind these was a kind, boyish face which was still handsome despite many years of anguish and sleep-deprived nights.

The third was somewhat of a mixture of the other two. He was middle-aged, middle in height and of middle achievement in the medical world. Subdued, balding and with ruined fingernails that gave away many years of dental abuse, Tom had trained in Scotland and now worked as a single-handed GP in Yorkshire. A failing practice, choked by bureaucracy and workload. He wore a blue Harris tweed jacket, long cheap trousers, and black Dr. Marten boots. Parts of him would have been passably fashionable in three different decades, but none at the same time, and certainly not in the current one. A light scar down his lip was the souvenir of an unsuccessful encounter with a cattle grid when he fell from his bike at the age of seventeen. And yet there was a visible, quiet defiance there too. He looked in deep thought as if he were planning something.

Because he was.

*

Four hours later, the same three men were sat separately in a pub on the corner of the street that heralded the entrance to the Medical Council's grand premises.

Dave was already on his second pint of beer and bowl of spicy nuts when Sid, stood a few metres away, nervously approached the barmaid, a mix of gentle cleavage, tattoos, and attitude. The barmaid, that was. Her name was Lexy, and for those that needed reminding, it was tattooed just above her natal cleft on her lower back. She was slim, pale-skinned, raven-haired and dangerous-looking. The type of woman your mother told you to avoid whilst secretly wishing she were just like her.

And yet, looks can deceive. Lexy was not all she seemed. Yes, she worked in a pub and could certainly turn heads, yet she yearned to study for a degree in classical literature, wrote poetry and had maintained her own motorbike until it had been stolen. Not that the customers ever cared to find this out. She was just 'Sexy Lexy' to her regulars and had been simply 'Lucy' to her parents.

"Excuse me, young lady, do you serve tea or coffee here?" Sid asked timidly. He hesitated. He was going to ask her something else. Dave was fascinated.

"And do you possibly have a phone charger I could use for a few minutes? I think my son's borrowed mine from my bag, and it's gone flat now. I'm happy to pay to borrow one for an hour. I hope you don't mind me asking?"

He tried to avoid looking at her cleavage. "A very pretty blouse," he said awkwardly as he caught her stare. He blushed.

She looked down. She was wearing a plain brown pub shirt with the logo across the pocket. The top button missing and a stain down the front. "It's my best one," she said with sarcasm.

"It's very… um… it suits you," replied Sid.

She eyed him suspiciously, mixed with an equal pub measure of irritation and intrigue. He was handsome in a neglected, world-weary sort of way. No wedding ring, she noticed. Unloved clothes. Terrible haircut. If he was married, the woman mustn't have loved him much at all. He looked back at her. A rabbit in headlights. A worried look on his face. She tried to look stern. Finally, with a slight smile, she shook her head and muttered to herself,

"Fuck me. A gent in my pub. There's a first."

"If that's a DiePhone you can borrow my lead," she added. "It'll fit. Just make sure you don't walk off with it or I'll... I'll pin you to the floor." And with that, she nipped around the back of the bar and put the kettle on. To her surprise, she had just blushed too.

Sid couldn't help following her lithe figure with his eyes as she turned around the corner. He stifled a transient sexual thought and felt immediately racked with guilt. Gosh, she's beautiful, he thought to himself. And he really meant it.

Sat in the corner, watching all three, was Tom. He was also on his second pint, but he nursed this one purposefully. A few minutes passed as he continued to study the two men from a distance. Their clothes. Their body language. And then finally, he stood up and spoke.

"Well, gents, have they had their pound of flesh from you two yet?" he asked in a quiet but authoritative voice that made Sid spill some of his newly made tea as he spun around in surprise. "There's a socket here for your phone and a good enough view of the local scenery to satisfy even you, Dr Rave." There was a startled flash of recognition from Dave as he looked into the corner at the face of Tom.

"Don't look so worried. I didn't marry her in the end." Tom said. "Not that you'd remember." A flash of guilty recognition followed.

"Tom? Tom from Donny General?" he spluttered. "Oh shit. Shit, I'm sorry. We were, um, very drunk. It was years ago. I don't even think she could remember the next day."

He continued to waffle unhelpfully, digging an ever-deeper hole for himself.

"I'm not interested," said Tom. "Ancient history. I'm not here to judge you. You were always a tart, Dave. I'm just intrigued to know why we three fine upstanding members of the medical community find ourselves facing a disciplinary hearing on the same day. There has to be some deep meaning to all this. And I'll offer a pint and a power socket to hear your stories. Serendipity, aided by its bastard child, The British Railway system, permits our storytelling. In case you didn't know already, all trains north are delayed by signal failure for hours. And I assume we're all heading north." He looked very serious for a moment. "Come with me if you want to live."

Dave laughed nervously, but the film reference was clearly lost on Sid, who simply looked more alarmed than ever. They both joined him at the table in the corner, however, and briefly shook hands. Then they sat down and chinked glasses and mug.

The conversation began, initially with social pleasantries and brief introductions, mainly for the sake of Sid. And then the stories began to be shared as the contents of the beer glasses and mug dwindled.

Tom was the first. Clear, matter of fact and without obvious emotion. Every third sentence accompanied by a sip of warm London beer and the occasional northern expletive about its temperature.

"So, I'm Dr Tom Lawrence, worked as a junior doctor with Dr Kildare here, and am now, or at least was until recently, a GP from Good old Donny. Doncaster to those in the know. Here's my sad but true story. Been there twenty-two years; single-handed, and used to love it. Great patients, not a bad area, despite the jokes, lovely staff, cheap housing and quite a mix of stuff medically. Then it all started to go to shit." He took a long gulp of beer and continued. "Home later and later each night. Holiday locum cover impossible to get. Kids starting to wonder who I was when I came through the door at night, at God-knows-what hour, usually carrying a carrier bag full of reports to finish off. The wife used to shout, then cry, then finally she just gave up altogether. I wasn't much fun to live with, and I started to numb it all away with a bottle of something from the Christmas drinks cabinet that the patients were kind enough to restock each December. Even the stuff that looked and tasted like mouthwash. It was empty by Easter this year, which was a personal record."

"Maybe it was mouthwash!" cracked Dave unhelpfully.

Tom shot him an irritated glance but then continued without another pause. "So finally, I've had a Thursday from hell. I'd stayed up half the night finishing reports and gone in, smelling of the Christmas mouthwash from the night before."

"So you were drunk on duty?" gasped Sid involuntarily in surprise.

"Not exactly, but I wasn't in a fit state to diagnose anything more complex than tonsillitis, depression or acne."

"So about 95% of the average GP clinic then," added Dave with a smile. Tom rolled his eyes. "And then some patient grassed you up?" Dave added, this time, attempting a more genuine look of concern, despite failing to fully conceal his grin.

"No. Well, sort of, but it gets worse. I'd done a crem form later that morning but forgotten about the patient's implanted defibrillator. I'd asked Dr Dozy-Bastard from the surgery down the road to do the part two, and he'd missed it completely too despite his 'thorough examination of the body' documented on the form."

"So what happened next?" asked Sid, with a genuine look of concern.

"Well, they attempted to incinerate the body at the local crem the following week and there was a rather loud bang."

"Oh fuck, I saw that on the news..." said Dave. "They thought it was a bomb."

"Yes, a cunning terrorist plot to murder the recently deceased," replied Tom with a wry smile.

"Anyway, the alcohol on my breath was recalled when they came to quiz my receptionist, and she's pathologically unable to lie. So here I am, suspended pending further investigations. On zero pay because I'm self-employed. Fucked in all senses."

"Except in the biblical," came the tennis shot return from Dave, unable to restrain his mouth in time. Tom ignored it.

"So that's my story. The road to ruin. And from a starting point in Doncaster, that takes some doing."

There was an awkward silence. And then Dave began to speak.

"Well, fathers, forgive me for I have sinned too. My story's pretty unfair really. I'm David Ravensberg. A Consultant Anaesthetist from Lancaster, and I'm divorced with three children who won't speak to me."

"Sorry to interrupt but did you by any chance shag one of your patients?" asked Tom. This time, with the first genuine smile he had managed in weeks.

"Of course not," protested Dave. He looked sheepish for a moment. "But they accused me of shagging the theatre sister in plastics."

"And did you, my son? Did you shag the theatre sister in plastics?" asked Tom in a hushed tone, adding, "Anyway, I thought that was part of an anaesthetist's job description." Tom now started to visibly brighten.

"I thought that was usually the surgeon's role," added Sid in such a quiet voice that neither of the other two heard him.

"So, did you?" asked Tom.

"Well, of course I did, but she was perfectly happy about it. But it turns out she was also the plastic surgeon's bit of fluff, too, so he reported me to the clinical director."

Sid said nothing.

"But they only had hearsay for evidence, surely?" asked Tom.

"Well, I'd forgotten they have CCTV cameras in recovery to keep an eye on the patients. They said I was bringing the hospital into disrepute," he added indignantly.

"Ah!" said Tom. "So you were both well and truly fucked!" At this, he let out a huge guffaw, and even Sid laughed, albeit mainly out of embarrassment. It was a therapeutic explosion for Tom, and he laughed until the tears streamed down his face.

"So there is poetic justice in this world, after all! That's hilarious. Got to be worth a pint, though." And he headed to the bar to order a refill.

"Here, you'll need this," he said as he handed Sid a pint of lager and sat down again. This time looking energised.

"I don't really drink alcohol..." protested Sid hesitantly. But then, as if to steel himself, he took a large gulp of the yellow liquid, pulled a face, and hesitantly began to speak.

"My name is Siddarth Ananthakrishnan, but no one can remember that, so I call myself Sid to fit in. I had an arranged marriage when I was thirty because my parents told me I was embarrassing the family in case I was gay. Which I'm not by the way... Not that I have any prejudice against..."

"We know, we know, get on with it," said Tom impatiently. He had followed Sid's gaze a few minutes ago, at the retreating barmaid.

"Well, my wife and I don't really spend very much time together except at functions. And she says I embarrass her. And I'm useless. And bad in the bedroom department." He looked visibly distressed for a moment. There was a pause, and the other two remained rapt and silent. "And so I made out a prescription for myself. For Sildenafil. I even prescribed the Viagra generically to save the local health authority some money."

"So the pharmacist shopped you?" asked Tom, looking serious.

"No, but I got a bad reaction and had to see my own GP, who is on the local ethical committee for the area LMC."

"Runny nose, red eyes?"

"Worse. Priapism," said Sid.

Now both colleagues collapsed into helpless laughter. So much so that the barmaid looked across at the three of them.

"It was really painful; I thought my penis would fall off. It was so hard and painful."

"Oh god, that is so funny. Yet poignant," said Dave.

"I was trying to prove to her that I am still a man," Sid added sadly. "But yes, I suppose there is a funny side to this too."

Tom finally managed to control his laugher and then attempted to look serious for a moment. "How long before it... you felt deflated?" He made a snort but composed himself again.

"Two days," said Sid. "I had to urinate in the bath," he added sadly.

Tom and Dave exploded into helpless laughter once again. "Welcome to the north of England. They've been doing that there for years!" said Dave.

Finally, Tom said, "Gentlemen." He lifted his glass. "I, Tom the crematorium explosives expert, Dave the surgical sister shagger and Sid, the eye poker-outer, are all destined to lose our medical licences to kill, after an incredibly long-winded investigation by our betters at the RMC, better known as the Ruin Medics' Careers."

"But surely it's their job to protect patients," said Sid.

"Bollocks, it's a gentlemen's club for maintaining their expensive carpets and whisky cabinets whilst providing knighthoods for the pompous few at the top," said Tom with visible disdain.

"But their second in command is a woman," added Sid, again quietly and almost to himself.

"Ok, one. And she's alright, but the rest of them are just bloody stooges for the Government and the minister of dark magic."

"The chief witch doctor," added Dave with a grin.

"Actually, traditional witch doctors try to heal people," said Sid. Again unheard.

"Yes, and I'm bloody sick of it," said Tom. "We'll be hung out to dry as 'bad examples' it's not fair. I've almost killed myself over this career."

"Very few doctors' children follow their parents into medicine these days," murmured Sid, sadly. "My son tells me he doesn't want to end up like me. I've worked so hard..." His sentence hung in the air.

Dave looked embarrassed.

"Actually, anaesthetics is quite a doss. At least it used to be. I've read loads of books during operations. Just don't take *Fifty Shades* into theatre with you. I was so engrossed one time, I didn't notice they'd finished the op. Good job the ODP was on the ball."

"So do we just accept our terminal career prognoses alone, or should we do something about it?" asked Tom.

"Like what?" asked Dave.

"Like get our own back. Here's my number. Let's keep in touch."

"Another pint, anyone?"

CHAPTER TWO: COOL AND CRAZY

It was Christmas 1991. The Doctors' Mess. Doncaster General Hospital. The music blared out of the large, otherwise bare room and a tacky cocktail of spilt drinks coated the floor. Smoke filled the air as a skinny young man stood awkwardly behind the rectangular table that was helpfully labelled 'the bar'. He wore a red Santa hat, trademark Doc Marten eight-hole boots and a t-shirt bearing a grinning wolf in shades on a surfboard, labelled 'cool and crazy'. Perhaps only the second statement was true.

He was surrounded by cans, cups, bottles of various coloured liquids, and there was a keg of beer to each side. Not the type of bar frequented by 007, perhaps, but it was functional. And very busy. A small group of student nurses giggled and gestured provocatively at the flustered barman as their co-conspirator stealthily slipped a bottle of vodka from the other side and hid it under her tinsel-covered skirt. Pre-poured beer was being handed out by the second helper, who didn't actually appear to be part of the official bar team at all. A headache of lights flashed incessantly whilst the steady thud of the base made the floor vibrate.

The dance floor itself was loosely located in the centre of the room and was already filled by a ragbag consisting mainly of drunken nurses, doctors, porters, cleaners and in fact, anyone who was attached to the hospital at all. Unbeknown to the ward staff, there were also a couple of absconded patients from the psychiatric assessment unit. They stood out from the others at the bar, as they were more coherent and articulate.

The night continued, and the young doctor behind the bar was clearly starting to flag when a pretty student nurse in a pink glittery top came straight up to him, leaned over the 'bar' and looked him straight in the eyes.

"I want your t-shirt," she declared. It wasn't a question; it was simply a demand. She held out her hand.

"It's my favourite t-shirt," he protested lamely, "What will I wear?"

She paused for a moment and then simply lifted her own t-shirt over her head and handed it to him.

"Here, this can be your souvenir for the night," she said and continued to hold her hand out impatiently. For a second, he simply stood and stared. She had a lovely slim figure, and he couldn't help but notice the small hearts embroidered on her bra. He knew her from the ward too. Suzie, they called her. He really liked her.

"You're not having that you cheeky bastard," she grinned, and he quickly handed over his t-shirt in embarrassment. He attempted in vain to turn hers inside out, so at least the glitter wouldn't show and then grabbed some spare tinsel off a passing reveller to camouflage his new apparel. He blushed crimson for the tenth or eleventh time that night, and threw back a pint of beer into which someone had festively added some spare Bacardi. He turned around, but she had gone. He felt deflated. It was chaos. It was Christmas in the doctors' mess. What would the Christ child have made of this?

"Your future in our fucking hands," Tom muttered to himself. But one hour and two pints of beer cocktail later, he was grinning inanely at the ceiling before abandoning the bar altogether to try to relocate the new owner of the cool and crazy t-shirt. His Doc Martens squelching in anticipation as he crossed the floor.

*

Meanwhile, approximately two hundred metres away, Dr Ravensberg was running across a car park as his cardiac arrest bleep wailed incessantly from his pocket. "This one better bloody well be ill," he snarled as he thought of the staff nurse he had left curled up in his on-call room. She only had a forty-five-minute break. He was wearing what appeared to be a cross between curtains and pyjamas but were actually termed 'theatre blues'. Loose-fitting, starchy and with a tendency to fall down at the least opportune moments, they at least had the advantage of being very quick to pull back on again. Which was very useful for crash calls occurring at inconvenient or anti-social times.

He ran through the fire door, down the corridor, and realised that ward 22 was the elderly medicine ward. Two lines of frightened, creased faces followed him as he dashed between the beds to the cubicle that was curtained off. He could hear a mix of nervous laughter and anxious, bellowed orders from behind the screen. He slowed to a brisk walk.

"Anaesthetist," he announced gallantly, as he pulled the curtain aside, "you can all relax now," and he went to the head end of the bed. A relieved-looking junior doctor handed him the bag and mask that she had been unsuccessfully attempting to resuscitate the elderly man with and stood aside.

"What's the story?" he asked the ward charge nurse, a weary-looking fifty-something with wiry grey hair and a face that had seen too much.

"Eighty-five-year-old male admitted with an MI last week. Seemed to be getting better 'til tonight. Said he wanted the bog and then... bang. So we called the Pontypandy Fire brigade, but you came instead. Not for the first time either, judging by those marks on your neck."

Dave was many things. He was shallow and vain. Self-centred and egotistical. But he was a good doctor and a skilled anaesthetist. And the atmosphere surrounding the bed had palpably calmed since his arrival.

"You're just jealous," he smiled. "Size eight and nine tubes, please, and a Larry Hagman with a decent light. Bernie, the throat please."

Bernard, the ODA hovering to his side, pressed down slightly on the poor man's Adam's apple, and the endotracheal tube was expertly passed through the limp vocal cords.

"Right, my terrified looking beauty, I want you to squeeze this bag like this," he said to the house officer lingering behind him. And he showed her how to gently ventilate the lungs with the oxygen passing through the rubber bag. He put his hand around hers to show her how firmly and quickly to squeeze the bag.

"What a gent," murmured the charge nurse with sarcasm.

"Just keep up the chest compressions. I imagine I'm singing 'I'm bad, I'm bad' in my head. It'll keep your timing about right." He winked at the house officer.

"I'm not really a Michael Jackson fan," she said, in return.

"Who's Michael Jackson?" grinned the anaesthetist.

The charge nurse rolled his eyes. "A man only marginally

more creepy than you, Dave."

"Right, where's the electricity?" Dave asked, changing the subject.

"On its way."

"Ok, let's pop a line in whilst we're waiting." He deftly inserted a green intravenous cannula into the elderly man's bulging external jugular vein, quickly withdrawing and offering a gift of a full syringe of blood which he intended to offer to the houseman, who had been struggling to get anything out of the man's limp arm.

"The internal jugular's better for proper central lines, but it's a quick way to get access," he explained to her.

"Tape, please. Want a few samples sending off with this? Pity to waste it… Um?"

"Jenny," she said.

"That was his mother's name," smirked the wired haired charge nurse.

"Was it really?" she asked Dave.

"No but it's a nice middle name for our first daughter."

She blushed.

There was a crashing sound like a mobile cutlery drawer being run over cobbles, as the defibrillator trolley finally arrived and was pushed through the curtain by a gasping, plethoric-looking porter, who had gone to the wrong ward twice as the unhappy result of a crackly pager and a simultaneous ear infection.

The elderly man was quickly wired up.

"Looks like VF on the monitor," said the charge nurse to Dave.

"Already charging," he replied, rather appropriately.

"Two hundred joules, please, and stand away from the bed if you wish to live 'til Boxing Day."

"Frankenstein… rise…" quipped Dave.

There was a sickening jolt as the elderly man jerked forward. Then a wait. Then nothing.

"Again?" asked the nurse.

"Yes but move your pads out a bit for the encore," said Dave.

He ignored the look he got in return, but the pads were duly moved further apart.

"Charging. Stand back."

Another jolt. This time there was a flatline. But then a definite heartbeat could be seen on the screen, followed by another. And miraculously, the elderly man slowly started to revive. His colour returned and he started to cough against the tube in his throat, which was duly removed.

"He's fucking Lazarus, blurted out the porter," and got a hard stare from the charge nurse who hissed tersely,

"There's elderly folk still alive out there, and they're not deaf!"

"Actually, most of them are," quipped Dave.

"Sorry," said the porter." I'm just relieved the old boy made it. I'll go." He looked embarrassed and apologetic.

And that was it. Bill, a retired merchant seaman and the survivor of two torpedo strikes in the North Atlantic convoys, got to live another three good years.

"You're a twat, Dave," said the charge nurse with a smile when they had finished. "But at least someone knows what they're doing here. You're our twat."

"I'm the cavalry," grinned Dave. "It's my job. I just try to calm everyone down, and you've got to admit, the team works better."

"Yeah, well, don't break any more hearts. Jenny's a good kid. She's got a boyfriend back home too."

"I've no idea what you mean," Dave grinned and turned to go back to his on-call room.

Just enough time for another bit of electricity between the sheets; then the Christmas party, if he still had the energy…

*

A young man sits quietly, cross-legged on a cushion. He is watching the scene in front of him with a mix of apprehension and despair, despite the colourful clothes and gentle music which threaten to overwhelm his senses. It is his sister's wedding. It is an arranged marriage, and he is the next child in line to be wed. He loves his family dearly and is the oldest boy. He is expected to lead and provide. He needs to maintain the family traditions and reputation. He needs to be married and have children. And yet, he craves to travel. To leave his town behind him and to explore the great wide world out there. He doesn't like the way his 'uncles' leer at the young girls in their saris. He doesn't like the corrupt police chief who is sitting next to his father. And he is embarrassed by the looks he is getting from his cousin and her friends, who look at him then turn back and giggle.

A fire glows, and the aroma of spice fills the air. The sky is full of stars, and insects chirp and whirr in the dark. Fireflies dance in a Brownian motion of flickering lights. In the distance, the chaos of a dangerous city is blanketed in soft yellow light.

"Another wedding in India," he sighs to himself. Life here in Kerala seems to revolve around the family and the potential to make more family.

"I see the fire in your eyes, Siddarth," whispers a voice just behind him. He turns with a start and sees the soft brown eyes of his cousin's friend, Priya, looking directly into his. Inquisitive. Intelligent. Bright. Reflecting the fire back.

"I think we need to escape", she says. "When do you finish your medical training?"

He looks back at her. Assured. Confident. Clever. Determined. And he has to admit, very pretty. She smells nice when she stands near him and he likes to hear her answer back when her brothers tease her and attempt to tell her what to do. She smokes. She makes him laugh. She seems the opposite of the child-bride being lined up for him. She is not wearing a sari. She is breaking tradition and wearing a western-style white dress. Her mother has already shouted at her. He has known her since childhood. They know each other's secrets and dreams. And so he replies, very quietly in case anyone is watching him,

"Yes. And soon," to both questions. "But I don't see how…"

"We marry each other and go to England or America," she says simply. "Then we live our own life out there. And do what we like."

Sid looks into her lovely eyes, breathes in her heady scent, and is silent for maybe a full minute. Then he simply says, "Yes."

But two additional sets of eyes have been watching the scene unfold. And now they are looking at each other, set with determination. This match will not be allowed.

CHAPTER THREE: ANGELS AND DEVILS

Three letters had arrived at three separate addresses that morning. The same type of impersonal, rather expensive, white envelope, completely anonymous save for the RMC herald on the reverse and containing a similarly bleak message to all three recipients.

Dear Doctor (Hand-Written Surname)

Following your preliminary disciplinary hearing at the RMC offices in Central London on the 14th of September 2018, it has been unanimously agreed that your medical registration should be suspended, pending further investigations.

We are unable to specify an exact timescale by when you will be informed of the outcome of these.

You are not allowed to accept any paid or unpaid medical work of any kind until the final outcome of this enquiry has been determined, and you should inform your employer and indemnity organisation immediately.

Your employer can organise a referral to the Occupational Health department to offer you further support in the meantime, should you wish to avail yourself of this.

There is an appeals procedure, details of which are available on the RMC website.

You should not cancel your direct debit to the RMC in the meantime, as payments for your annual subscriptions will continue to be requested from your designated bank account, as usual. Cancellation will result in your permanent removal from the medical register, as detailed in our terms of service.

Yours sincerely
(Illegible squiggle with a noticeable flourish at the end)

On behalf of the RMC

The three letters received three distinctly different reactions from their recipients.

The first recipient exploded in a tirade of Anglo Saxon expletives, mostly doubting the parentage and mode of conception of its senders. After a while, the first recipient slumped back in his chair, seemingly exhausted. He closed his eyes and held his head in his hands, rocking slightly as he did so. Finally, he stood up and walked to his drinks cabinet. He picked up the heaviest bottle of scotch he could find. And with enormous vitriol, he hurled it at the wall, upon which his medical certificates and multiple post-graduate diplomas were displayed. The sound of disintegration was terrifying.

Later still, he poured the contents of every other bottle down the toilet, swept up the splintered debris, placed a new picture over the dent in the wall, and filled his blue recycling bin with empty bottles. There was a lot.

The second letter was received in a quiet, dignified and absolutely defeated way, having already been opened by its recipient's spouse, who was now deftly targeting a barrage of insults and threats at him. She explained in detail how useless and unevolved he was from primordial slime. He sat and absorbed the verbal (and occasionally physical) missiles for around ten minutes and then simply stood up, gathered his spectacles, wallet, and car keys, and walked out of the house. He didn't look back, but he could hear further salvos narrowly missing their target as he continued to walk towards the one possession that he had chosen for himself. Fortunately, he always kept his passport in the boot, along with a sleeping bag.

And yet, the third letter was received quite differently again. Its owner opened the envelope, gave a wry smile, shrugged his shoulders, and started to search the internet for flights.

"Fuck 'em. Holiday time," he said simply. He then carefully pinned the note to his dartboard and threw a dart straight through the crest on the letterhead. It was a good shot.

*

Meanwhile, back at a public house in central London, the barmaid was polishing glasses. The usual mix of clientele was in the bar - a couple of Japanese tourists, very polite and photographing everything from beer mats to fire exit signs. Then the regulars, unhealthy looking specimens, with pale skin, distended abdomens, and poorly concealed lecherous looks. And finally in the corner, a duo who had walked in from the nearby RMC building. The first, a skinny man of about forty, moustached and nervous-looking. He wore an anaemic looking suit, an effeminate tie, and sharp Italian shoes. Definitely gay, she thought. The only man in here who admires my shoes instead of my arse. Then there the second man: well-nourished, greasy skinned and wearing an expensive dark suit and spotted red bow tie with a silk handkerchief protruding from the top right pocket, next to a Waterman type pen. Left-handed and right-wing, mused Lexy. She had seen them both many times before. The Chuckle Brothers, as she had nicknamed them. Today, they were clearly in some kind of deep conversation. Bowtie man was clearly the more dominant conversationalist of the two. He was attempting to emphasise a point without raising his voice. All Lexy could hear was, "... Minister says got to make a bloody example of …threats to close us down... cuts... bloody GPs… private… coming in anyway… Or it'll ruin my bloody Honours nomination," he finished with a flourish. She got the gist.

She despised him. She was pretty astute, and she had immediately sensed a queasy mix of self-importance, inadequacy, and a desire to dominate others when she had first seen him. She didn't like the way he looked at her, at her tattoos in particular, and the lack of any attempt to hide his sheer sense of superiority. She saw a lot of men in her bar. Most were polite enough, most were inadequate. Some clearly had a thing for tattoos. But none treated her with such a level of visible disdain as he did. No one asked her anything about herself at all. Except for her name. Or her phone number.

"My round," announced bowtie man grandly, and he sauntered up to the bar. Lexy attempted a smile… unsuccessfully.

"I'll have a whisky, a decent malt mind, and my colleague would like a tomato juice. And then whatever your heart would desire for yourself, my dear."

She suppressed the visual image that followed and simply said, "Thank you, but I'm fine."

"It's ok, it's on expenses," said the customer with a leary grin.

"I'm not. Still no, but thank you anyway," she replied firmly. God, he was a creep.

As he walked back to the corner, she couldn't help but notice the anxious look from the other man in the corner. He looked exquisitely uncomfortable. He clearly wasn't at all interested in her, but he kept looking around him for anyone else in the bar.

You two are up to no good, thought Lexy. Whatever you're up to, you're not keen to be overheard...

A regular interrupted her thoughts. "Oi, any fackin' chance of a beer this week, darlin'?"

"Why are men all such pricks?" she mumbled to herself as she turned around to face the yellowing face of her oldest regular.

She smiled, "Of course, usual Bob?"

And with that, she hastened his hepatic demise with another two or three units of ethanol.

*

Sid was sat in his car, with the engine idling. He had pulled into the McDonald's drive-thru and was now waiting for one of the few vegetarian options on the menu to be specially cooked for him and brought to the waiting bay where he had parked. He had a cup of hot chocolate in one hand and an old photo on his front seat. His phone was almost flat once again, and the charger lead had been borrowed by his son.

He had been quietly crying for a while, and at first, didn't hear the gentle knocking on his window. He was lost in thought. Of Priya, of his family back in Kerala. Of the end of his medical career. Of how to quietly kill himself without invalidating his life insurance for his wife and child. He prayed that it would soon be all over. The gentle knocking became a little more insistent.

"Sir, your order." She was a round-faced girl with pulled-back hair and gentle blue eyes. Her badge indicated that she was called Angela, and as she saw Sid's face, she could see his red eyes and running nose.

"Here, you might need some of these," she said kindly. She gave him a handful of white serviettes. "They're really absorbent, thank God." She handed him his food and then hesitated. "You might not remember me, doctor, but you once looked after me when I lost my baby. I'll never forget you, cos you didn't make me feel stupid like the others did. You just listened." She paused and looked at his puffy red eyes. "Whatever's wrong, it'll be ok. Good things come to good people in the end."

And with that, she leant into the car and kissed him gently on the forehead; then she was gone. It was a simple act. But it was a touch of human contact and kindness that Sid hadn't experienced for a very long time indeed. The tears came again, in torrents, but these ones felt warmer. Finally, he glanced at his phone, which had buzzed, and noticed that a new message had appeared. It was from Tom. It simply said: *FANCY A CERVEZA OR TWO IN TENERIFE SID? THEY DO TEA THERE TOO. PHONE ME IF YES, AND STILL PHONE IF NO, 'COS DAVE BOUGHT US TICKETS AND YOU OWE HIM EIGHTY QUID. PS DON'T GO AND DO SOMETHING DAFT IN THE MEANTIME.*

There was a second message. It was from Dave.
I NEED YOUR PASSPORT DETAILS IF YOU'RE COMING SID.

The Crash Team

FULL NAME, EXPIRY DATE (YOUR PASSPORT NOT YOURS) AND PASSPORT NUMBER. PLUS PREFERENCE FOR TYPE OF AIR HOSTESS.

Sid wiped his eyes and actually managed a smile. He blew his nose and thought about it for a few minutes. He was pretty healthy generally, and so his sudden unexpected death would be bound to end up in further toxicology testing, where the cocktail of tablets he has been planning to take would undoubtedly be detected. More shame on his family and no pay-out would follow either. He hadn't been away for a long time either. And so he typed back *OK* and then checked for his passport. The message sent, his DiePhone battery gracefully expired.

Just when he was starting to panic, he managed to find a pound coin down the back of the seat, which was fortunate, as his wallet had been emptied of cash earlier that day by his wife. He looked across the car park at a row of shops. A 99p shop made a beckoning smile. It would sell charger leads, and they could even keep the change. With that, he finished his McVeg and opened his car door.

Angela watched him through the window and smiled to herself. She wasn't quite sure what had come over her but hoped it had helped a little. He was a nice man. Quite dishy too.

CHAPTER FOUR: BUDGET WINGS AND BUDGIE SMUGGLERS

Manchester Airport Terminal 3. The three men sat in the waiting area of the rather less ornate building, filled with plastic chairs, MDF panels and tired industrial carpet. It was two days since the first text message had been sent. The terminal at Manchester Airport was steadily filling with a mix of the bored, the hyperactive and the plain aerophobic. Sid was the first to speak.

"Thank you for organising this, but do we actually have a plan?"

Since the bottle recycling episode, Tom had stopped drinking altogether and felt a mixture of relief, vague craving, and nausea. He now also sported a slight tremor, which he hoped wasn't too noticeable. "Of course," he replied with a meaningful look. "But I now need your help to complete the master plan and improve it from its current status of only 'quite brilliant' into becoming the best plan since Mr Hovis watched his wife hacking at the loaf with a blunt knife for the last time."

Sid had no plan at all, and so anything was progress as far as he could see. He had spent the last two days avoiding the multitude of missed calls, texts, and insults that he knew would now be awaiting him if he switched it back on. He had simply texted his practice manager to say: *I AM SAFE BUT NOT ABLE TO COME BACK TO WORK FOR A LONG TIME. PLEASE TELL THE CCG9 THEY NEED TO PROVIDE A LONG-TERM LOCUM AND GIVE EVERYONE MY VERY BEST REGARDS. I AM SO SORRY.* Then he texted his son to ask him to look after the family whilst he was away and to promise to do his homework and help around the house. And to say that he loved him.

"Well," announced Tom, "the brilliant plan starts with a week or two near a pool and ends with justice. There's only the middle bit missing," he admitted. "But it's a work in progress."

"We did think about launching a Scud missile at the RMC's records department but then realised we'd used the last one up."

Sid thought for a moment. "David, I hope you don't mind me saying something that may offend you. I notice that you have an eye for a pretty girl."

Tom snorted with laughter.

"He's had more shags than we've had shits!"

Sid looked extremely uncomfortable.

"Well, I just wondered if the lady on the reception desk at the council may be open to a little of your charm? She might hold the key, so to speak?"

They both looked at him. There was a short pause.

"Sid, you are officially the new Head of Intelligence at our new University for No Hopers. Dave can be appointed Head of Cunning in the Language Department. He's good at cunning lingo."

Dave actually looked rather pleased with the whole idea.

"So part one of our brilliant plan is conceived, and we haven't even got past the boarding gate."

"Hopefully, the only conception," added Sid and all three laughed. Sid, it seemed, was not only the sharpest tool in this particular box but also had a sharp sense of humour.

"I used to be considered funny once," he added, with a self-deprecating smile.

"Sid, you are officially funny again. You'll be putting whoopee cushions under the pilot's seat before we know it."

And with that, boarding was announced.

*

Sid had been thinking for the whole flight, whilst Tom had snored, and Dave spent most of his time looking longingly at the hostess. The airline food had been surprisingly palatable. Just finding and stealing their records wouldn't work. He wasn't sure how they would be backed up on the computer, and it was inherently dishonest, which bothered him. It also didn't address their need to be reinstated if they wanted to practice medicine again, although he was starting to doubt if he would ever want to.

Tom was dreaming. He was back at the bar at the Christmas party. Everywhere there were people dancing, drinking, and swaying from side to side. The pretty nurse was approaching him. She started to lift her top up, but this time another pair of arms embraced her and pulled her away. She was soon lost in the crowd, and as Tom moved forward to find her, he found himself being held back by the legs. He looked down and saw his cool and crazy t-shirt wrapping around his legs, tighter and tighter. The revellers were now laughing at him and he was falling into the slops bucket. He could taste the sour beer and spirits. And then he awoke with a start. He was clammy and could feel his heart pulsing in his chest. His coat had somehow wrapped around his legs, and Sid was trying to help him.

"Tom, you don't look well," he said kindly. "Do you mind me asking if you need help with something? You are shaking."

Tom looked at the gentle, concerned face that looked at his. "Do you think perhaps you need a small drink and some food?"

It was pointless pretending to him.

"Sid, I drink way too much. I didn't always, and I really don't even like the taste of most of it. But I honestly don't think I'd have survived the last two years without it." He paused. "I've had nothing for nearly three days now, and I'm starting to feel really shit. What do you suggest, doctor?"

Sid looked at him. Tom looked tired and weary of life. His jowls were swollen, and Sid guessed that his parotid salivary glands were reacting negatively to their daily poisoning. His skin was pallid, and his lower abdomen looked swollen.

"If you were my patient, Tom, I'd tell you that I think you need to cut down more gradually," he said. "You need to eat some proper food and take some vitamins too. Otherwise, you are in danger of having a seizure. I hope you don't mind me telling you the truth. I think that's what you'd tell yourself."

Tom looked at Sid. "You're right," he said. "I'm even a bloody failure at stopping drinking."

"You are just unhappy," said Sid. "Your nails are worse than my uncle's."

Tom retracted his hands from view.

"But you will be ok. We need your ideas. The brilliant plan is not yet brilliant enough. Here."

He handed Tom a small bar of chocolate that he had also found in his car. It was out of date but still edible.

"I'd buy you a drink, but I think they're only taking cash. I suggest a small beer now and maybe a bottle of duty-free that you don't like for when we get there. We'll divide it into doses."

"Ok," said Tom. "Good plan. I'll get rum. I absolutely hate

the stuff. Memories from a very bad night out in student days."

"Vitamins will have to wait, I'm afraid."

An hour later, he was looking somewhat better. He'd managed to consume almost all of an airline meal that had consisted of the smallest chicken curry he had ever seen, followed by a tiny slice of cake and some cheese and biscuits. The beer had tasted bitter, and he really hadn't enjoyed it but realised that Sid was right about the risk of him getting the full-blown DTs and having a fit. Later, he slept again, but this time in his dream, she had swapped t-shirts with him, and they were now holding hands on a beach. Sid watched him for a while before returning to his own thoughts.

Meanwhile, Dave was chatting to one of the stewardesses, and Sid saw her hand him a piece of paper with something written on it. He was an absolute bugger, thought Sid, but he was certainly the man they needed for the first part of the plan. Dave sat down again, grinning broadly from ear to ear.

"Sid, I think I'm in love with the trolley dolly from heaven. She's called Misha, and she's from Russia."

"Very James Bond," said Sid with a smile. "Though I prefer 'On her Majesty's Secret Service'. I saw that as a child back in India. Through a fence panel, believe it or not. It's a love story too. Bond gets married in it. Not for very long though, unfortunately."

"She's even written me a message in Russian after her number," said Dave, who wasn't listening. "Look."

He proudly handed Sid the love epistle. Sid looked at the note, written in beautifully neat Russian, and struggled not to laugh. *Sorry, Casanova you're too old for me, please pass my number to your son,* it translated as. He suspected that the number would be even more of a disappointment. Maybe her great aunt? Sid had studied Russian back at school in India. He could see the other stewardesses giggling at the far end of the plane.

"What a surprise," he said tactfully and handed it back. Perhaps they might need a back-up plan after all.

*

A poolside in Tenerife

The following day, two pinking bodies lay next to the darker skin of the third on three adjacent sunbeds. The first was furtively gazing around the apartment pool at the only two topless women, sunbathing at the opposite end. Dave guessed that they must be either Dutch or Scandinavian. Spanish girls were unlikely to sunbathe, either at this time or in this way. He couldn't identify their language either.

The resort was lively, noisy, and mostly budget, with a small, original centre and a sprawl of poorly planned development. The heavy thud of music drowned out the tranquillity of an autumn day, and cigarette smoke drifted lazily over the scene, creating a light smog. Sid was intermittently in deep thought again, whilst also passing occasional glances at the topless duo, followed by an exaggerated attempt to look around the complex at everything else too, to avoid being considered a voyeur. Tom was simply asleep. Aided by the single dose of rum that he had taken an hour earlier. God, it was awful stuff but it had stifled the shakes somewhat. An hour later, Sid gently shook Tom.

"I think you are burning, Tom. Would you like me to get you some sun cream?"

"Good plan, have you got any?" he looked at Sid's dark skin and then realised the stupidity of his own question.

"Um, Dave. Have you got any? Sun cream, that is? As it looks like one side of you is burning too."

Dave looked at him with a grin. "I reckon they're

Norwegian. Those girls over there." He made a cringe-worthy gesture. Subtlety was not Dave's forte. "They're looking over here now and then and giggling. I think we should go over and say hello. Introduce ourselves."

Tom looked over and waved. "They're a bit young for you, Dave." The girls waved back. "I think they're checking you're still alive. They're also Welsh. And I think they're on their honeymoon. I passed them in the lift earlier."

Dave looked aghast. Sid laughed. He knew that this apartment complex didn't have a working lift. Tom was regaining his sense of humour. Tom was also right about them being Welsh. The bag with the red dragon being the clue. Tom also understood a few words of Welsh, including *diawl budur*, which the darker haired girl had used a couple of times to describe Dave. Dave beckoned them over.

A few minutes later, they were all chatting at the poolside bar. Ann and Rhiannon had been briefed by Tom and were now holding hands whilst giggling. It was happy hour, although the barman's face camouflaged this well.

"*Tres Cervezas grandes y dos colas light, por favor, mi amigo,*" breezed Dave. "*Y un crocodillo queso.*"

"'Ow many straws mate?" responded the barman in a strained cockney accent, followed by a genuine grin.

"You're from London!?" replied Dave.

"*No Señor,* Madrid, but I like to tell good joke!" he beamed this time and introduced himself. "*Diego, Señor.* And your Spanish is not bad! But we have no bandages left, so I will serve you a '*bocadillo con queso*'." He made a crocodile gesture with his hands and this time they all laughed at Dave's error. Tom could see that the idea of the ladies being a couple had not put Dave off at all.

"So, I hear congratulations are in order," he said. They briefly looked at each other in surprise.

"Dave means on your wedding," prompted Tom, with a wink.

There was a brief pause. "Oh yes, very romantic," said Ann, the fair-haired one. She was in her mid-twenties, quite fair-skinned and had a pretty, lively face. "We got married here and went home for a honeymoon."

"In Rhyl," added Rhiannon, with a longing gaze at Ann. Sid stifled a guffaw.

"They're not very open to us being a gay couple in Wales, so we've come here instead," said Ann with a straight face.

"Except in Bangor," added Rhiannon with a shriek of laughter. Diego looked at Ann in astonishment.

"You never tell me you are gay!" he exclaimed. And that was it. They both laughed like drains for a good five minutes. Sid and Tom joined in until tears streamed down their faces.

And out came the true story. Ann and Rhiannon hailed from North Wales and were holiday reps, working in a local family apartment complex. Ann looked after the younger children's club whilst Rhiannon organised pool and evening activities. They were friends. Ann was going out with the barman. And Rhiannon was single again after having her heart broken by the karaoke engineer. She was curvier than Ann and had a small tattoo of a dragon on her left shoulder. She smiled at Sid as she saw him gazing at it. He blushed slightly. They had become great friends whilst working together and were fed up with being chatted up by drunken and mostly married Englishmen, whose kids were in the 'little sharks club'.

"In training for adulthood, no doubt," remarked Tom, with irony.

And they shared an apartment in this block as it was the cheapest in the area, owing to an ongoing cockroach and stray cat infestation, keeping the prices competitive. Sid and Tom both looked at Dave.

"The feedback wasn't that bad on the internet," he countered lamely.

"I would not let my cat stay here..." added Diego.

Ann gave him a stare. "He doesn't have a cat," she added. "He has a tiger. Me!"

Dave was just about to retort with a crass comment about caring for stray pussies when he was interrupted by Tom, who had been genuinely amazed by the transformation of the deadpan barman to Ken Dodd challenger. Diego must have overheard at least some of Dave's earlier lecherous comments, directed at his girlfriend, but didn't seem to hold a grudge. Tom looked longingly at one of the beers before taking another gulp of cola light, followed by an involuntary belch, combined with a sneeze. Sid smiled too. But this time, he was starting to drift away in his own thoughts again. They all carried on laughing and talking, but Sid's thoughts drifted further and further.

He missed his son, despite not having to look for his phone charger every lunchtime. And he missed caring for his patients, who were mainly elderly and frail. He looked over at the elderly couple holding hands on adjacent sunbeds. His son hadn't responded to any attempts at contact since Sid had been suspended.

His thoughts moved on. This time to a man in his eighties who had presented to his colleague a few weeks earlier with sudden onset back pain and "pain when I take a leak or stand up, doc." The pain was new, but the urinary leak problem hadn't been. In fact the 'leak' had been a red herring altogether. The man had split the wall of his abdominal aorta, and Sid had only spotted this when the man's blood pressure had started to fall precipitously the following day at the second home visit he attended. He had died shortly afterwards, and Sid wished he had become involved earlier in his care. He looked so like the elderly man across the pool.

The same colleague had also missed a clot within a bowel artery of an elderly woman a few weeks earlier, whom he had said "probably has a grumbling appendix." She had died of surgical complications after Sid had admitted her a few days later with a gangrenous bowel. He was still racked with guilt. What would happen now he wasn't there? He knew that he couldn't return to work, even if he had wanted to, but he blamed himself. He hadn't shopped his senior colleague out of a sense of loyalty and seniority but realised that he couldn't cover up for him now.

He also hadn't told Tom and Dave his own full story, and he harboured a sense of profound guilt about this. It wasn't his wife for whom he had tried to reawaken his libido and self-confidence. It was for a lovely drugs rep, for whom he had developed somewhat of an infatuation. She had invited him to a conference, and he hoped that she secretly longed to be with him. He had wanted to tell her that he thought she was beautiful and interesting, but she had spent the whole evening flirting with a garrulous professor from London instead.

In fact, Sherry from Anglo-pharma was hoping for a leg up in her career rather than a leg over. She liked Sid, and had noticed his shy interest in her, but her interest in him was purely career-based. Lonely bloke, well connected, she thought to herself. Similarly, Professor Queasy from Chelsea was pretty awful, but at least he was looking for an opening for a PA in his private rooms on Harley Street. Although she was pretty sure she knew what type of opening he was looking for.

His thoughts bounced from his sense of impotency as a man to his impotency to challenge his colleague, when a Yorkshire accent awoke him from his reverie. It was Tom.

"Sid, Sid. Are you still with us, mate? Coming in for a swim?" he asked. "I need waking up. And Rhiannon here thinks you're nice. She's also decided that she's no longer gay."

Rhiannon gave Tom a sharp look.

"Dave, on the other hand, will need to remove the beak from his budgie smugglers if he is to be allowed back in the pool..."

"The S's have also fallen off his Speedos."

This time they all laughed, expect Diego, who didn't understand the joke. Sid looked back at Dave and Tom with fondness. Dave was the butt of much of Tom's humour, but there was no obvious malice in the comments, and Dave took the jibes good-naturedly. They clearly liked each other, despite their past clash. Oddly enough, this ramshackle group of people with their varied, car-crash backgrounds were becoming friends. They shared a common bond despite their differences.

"Ok," said Sid to his latest patient. "Swim, followed by your afternoon dose."

"Dave will probably have acquired a dose of something else by then," Tom grinned back.

"Well, not from me he won't," replied Rhiannon indignantly, with a wink at Sid.

Dave looked at Tom. "What's he got that I haven't?"

"Oh Dave, where to begin?" Tom answered quietly to himself.

*

The afternoon had been fun. Even Diego had eventually joined them in the pool when his shift had ended. They'd played a drowning-come-volleyball game, and the girls ensured that their tops stayed firmly on despite Dave's best efforts to dislodge them. Sid was clearly unable to catch or hit a ball straight, but Tom and Dave were surprisingly agile. Similarly, Ann was quite the athlete, owing to her stamina, coordination and aided by her having previously represented Colwyn Bay in the Welsh under-18s water polo league. Diego was competitive, whilst Rhiannon was happy to simply splash and laugh at the others.

"You're so competitive!" she kept saying to Dave.

A few around the pool were watching and smiling, and a few even joined in. It was silly, and fun and exhilarating. And escapist. Tom looked ten years younger by the time he had finished.

"We're heading back in for a shower. Maybe see you old guys later?" asked Rhiannon with a smile.

"That depends," said Tom. "Let me check our diaries… ok we're free from 6:30pm until… 2028, so we can just about squeeze you in." He smiled. He felt eighteen again. The poolside returned to peace. All three were now lying in the shade, chatting intermittently. The light was starting to fade.

"Sid, why did you become a doctor then?" asked Dave, with genuine interest once the girls had left the poolside.

"Because I was top of my class," replied Sid. "And my parents wanted me to. Otherwise, it was pharmacy, law, or engineering. But I don't regret it. I like medicine. The patients are mostly very kind. I like helping them."

"How about you?" he asked in reply.

"I suppose the same reasons," said Dave. "Well, also because I hoped I might be able to get a girlfriend. I was pretty hopeless with the ladies at school."

"Which school?" asked Sid.

"It was a local comprehensive. I think I was their first straight-A student in years. The headmaster told me it was my duty to enhance the school's reputation."

"What did you want to be then?"

Dave looked embarrassed for a moment. "Promise you won't laugh, but I wanted to be an actor on the telly."

Tom snorted on his sunbed.

"So how about you, teetering-on-the-teetotal Tom?" asked Dave, a little harshly. "A barman?"

"I was a barman for a while actually," replied Tom. "I worked in Yorkshire during the summer of the coalminer's strike. They told me they only took me on so I could sort out the barmaids' 'women's problems'. I was a second-year student at the time. I hadn't even learnt the anatomy of the perineum at the time."

"How did you get on?" asked Sid.

"Honours in Gynaecology three years later," laughed Dave. "Sorry, cheap shot from me." But the previous tension was gone.

"Ah, I deserved it," said Tom. "I'm always taking the piss. Need to be able to take it too."

"So what next?" asked Sid. "Any more ideas yet?"

"I'm still thinking," replied Tom. "How much do you know about IT, gents?"

"Not much," admitted Dave. "I just about manage at work. The important stuff. Google your diagnosis, eBay, Amazon, Doctor Bukk Teef…"

"Me too," said Sid. "I nearly got suspended for emailing a photo of my patient's mole to every GP in the region."

"Why the problem? And how the hell did you manage that?" asked Tom.

"Well, it was on her breast, and it was a pre-set list. I hit the wrong button and didn't realise they'd all get a copy!"

"Weren't all the names listed?"

"No, I meant to send it to the dermatology department."

"And who received it, Sid?"

"Derbyshire's general practitioners," answered Sid quietly. "All of them."

"You must have felt a right tit," said Dave with sincerity.

"It may have been a left one," added Tom. They both snorted with schoolboyish laughter. Sid looked very embarrassed.

"So you two IT wizards aren't much help then," said Tom, when he'd managed to stop laughing. "The power of a misdirected email, eh?!"

"We're only doctors. We rely on our children for help with IT matters," added Sid.

It was a throwaway comment, but that second remark of Sid's set Tom's brain off again. He paused for a minute. And then said, "Sid, or may I call you Dr Watson?" and he smiled again. "I, in the meantime, will be Holmes!"

CHAPTER FIVE: WISH YOU WERE HERE?

It was a cold, drizzly day in London a few days later. Lexy was cleaning the glasses at the side of the bar and awaiting the usual mix of testosterone and cirrhosis that the striking of twelve o'clock would surely summon. Earlier she had cleared the few bits of rubbish and lost property that had accumulated over the past twenty-four hours and left it all in a carrier bag behind the bar. She was feeling reflective. Last night, she had discovered that her on-off boyfriend of the past two years had been sleeping with a girl he had met on the internet, and the row that had followed had been brief but very physical. He had denied it angrily initially and then reacted with fury when confronted with his web browsing history and deleted voicemails.

Why are men so stupid and predictable, she thought? He'd seemed perfectly ok at the start. But then he was just 'her type'. The type she had dated since the age of sixteen. Handsome. A bit rough. Charming. Practised at chat-up lines. And good in bed. Again, no doubt from practice. She was approaching thirty now. Engaged once, and hoping to have a family of her own, to make up for her own lack of family. Fostered and then adopted from the age of six, all she knew of her natural family was that she was one of many children and had been neglected at the least and abused in other ways at the worst.

Her tattoo had appeared when she was just sixteen and was mainly to demonstrate rebellion against her adoptive parents, who were kind but strict, elderly and conservative with a big 'C'. Her adoptive father had died when she was nineteen and her mother a few years later. Mainly of a broken heart, she thought. She had briefly been to college to start a hairdressing course at the behest of her father but had changed to motorcycle maintenance shortly after and discovered a love of bikes. No one would take her seriously as a mechanic, and so she drifted from job to job; initially in retail sales, but she was dismissed after telling a particularly rude woman that she could "shove her American Express gold card right up her flabby arse". Never a good sales pitch to the shop's best customer. The "flabby" comment seemed to have caused the most offence.

Pub jobs had followed and then a night course in IT security, which she had genuinely enjoyed. But again, the lack of references on her CV, in fact, the lack of a CV altogether, stopped her potential career in its tracks.

She was disturbed by a knock at the door. The postman. With the usual flyers, bills, and a postcard.

"Are you Lexy the Landlady?" he asked. "Postcard for you." He handed her the card. It had a Spanish donkey on the front and was stamped 'Los Cristianos'. She cautiously turned the card over.

Wish you were here? Thanks for the loan of your charger to our good knight. Sid would send his love but is far too shy.

Pool at the El Ole cold. Beer warm. Bring your factor 20.

Love, the RMC garbage refugees, aka the 3 amigos!
Tom Dave Sid xoxox

She laughed out loud. The cheeky buggers. She assumed that Tom was the one who had sat in the far corner that afternoon, and Dave was the ageing Lothario. She remembered Sid, though. After she had lent him the charger, he had also noticed the tattoo on her left arm which read, 'never regret anything that once made you smile'. After the other two had left, they had ended up discussing modern literature, which had been both invigorating and rather weird. He was kind and self-effacing. Very different from her usual clientele. He was also surprisingly athletic-looking for his age. She assumed he swam or ran.

In fact the gym was Sid's refuge from his family. He simply sat in the lounge drinking tea much of the time and reading books. Many of which he absentmindedly left behind before he had managed to finish them. He liked romances and stories of heroism and escape the most.

The second noise was a commotion.

"Now then, young lady, I'm sure I've left something in here. Unless your cleaner has managed to lose it already."

She bristled. Lexy was also the cleaner. "And what have you lost exactly?" she asked the man coolly, whom she immediately recognised as being from the RMC offices across the road.

"Just a file. Nothing important but a fawn-coloured file with some papers in it."

Lexy took a look in one of the bags she had filled the previous day. Spectacles, a well-thumbed, scruffy paperback. "Not this then?" She held out the book.

"Certainly not," he said indignantly. It was a novel with a pornographic cover. She tried not to smile. A couple of old magazines. A coffee shop points card.

"No sorry, but if you give me a contact email and phone number, I'll see what I can do when I next speak to the cleaner. Your name?"

He gave her his name, email and contact number and left without another word.

"No drink on expenses for me today then?" she said to herself. "Creepy bastard." And then she carefully put the second bag next to her own. She'd have a little peek inside that before she handed it back to its rightful owner.

"Oy, any fackin' chance of a beer this week, darlin'?" A voice broke her concentration.

"Oh fuck off you, old drunk," she replied with a volleyed return before turning round to find herself looking into the shocked eyes of her boss, stood next to her old regular.

There was a long silence. Lexy paused for a minute. And then without another word, turned, picked up her handbag, phone, charger lead, the second lost property bag and finally, the postcard.

"Sorry, life's just too short to take this shit anymore," she finally said. "Bob, you're killing yourself. Get a life before it gets you. Gawp at your own wife's tits for a change. I resign."

And with that, she walked out of the Wolf and Whistle for the last time. Bob and Bill simply gurned in silence at each other.

*

Back at the RMC office, the man with the bow tie was starting to look flustered.

"Which bloody idiot moved the file?" he demanded accusingly of the secretary sat at the mahogany reception desk.

Beads of sweat pooled at the corners of his forehead. He removed his jacket, and dark clouds were forming on his shirt, under each armpit. He had been searching feverishly and unsuccessfully for thirty, increasingly irritable minutes.

"Is it the brown file you took out yesterday to the meeting with the minister?" she inquired innocently. "I didn't notice you bring it back in the carrier bag you took it out in...."

She heard him curse quietly.

Serves you right, you nasty little creep, she thought to herself. "Can I do anything to help?" She added with a faux look of concern. "I'm sure it'll turn up somewhere. Probably where you least expect it."

"That's what I'm bloody well afraid of," he murmured again to himself.

He sat down. A look of despair on his face. Then he remembered the bag. It was the Harrods bag that he used to shop at the cheaper supermarkets. He'd seen Lexy look into the same kind of bag only an hour or so earlier.

"That skinny, conniving bitch..." he exclaimed. His secretary looked around sharply. "Not you, the barmaid at The Whistle..."

Oh, that's ok then! Lucky girl, she fumed inwardly. Good old Lexy, she thought. She knew exactly who he meant. Hope the old bastard gets what he deserves. She used to pop into the pub at the end of her shift sometimes, and she liked her. Lexy was a breath of fresh air.

Bowtie man left the building. He walked straight to the pub, with the malignant intent of having Lexy sacked on the spot. He knew Bill, the manager, well. Bill helpfully added several bottles to the bills of the larger RMC events, and shared these with him on a fifty-fifty basis. Decent chap that he was. As he arrived, he found Bill behind the bar, fumbling desperately with the modern digital till.

"Bollocks," said Bill in despair.

"Where's that barmaid of yours?" asked bowtie man.

"She's facked off," added yellow Bob with genuine misery. "And he can't operate the fackin' till". He pointed at the only other person in the pub, to emphasise his point.

"Did she have a Harrods bag with her?"

"Fink she took some stuff, but don't know what," replied yellow Bob helpfully.

"It's your bloody fault she left in the first place, Bob," added Bill, whilst frantically hitting multiple keys on the till.

A minute passed. Bowtie was now searching behind the bar. He didn't find the Harrods bag, but he was pretty sure she'd found it already. His well-thumbed book was still in the bin.

"Any chance of a beer?" came a voice from the other side.

"Oh bugger off will you, we're busy," responded bowtie man without turning around.

"God, it's like being in the Commons bar," replied the voice and the Minister for Health took a seat behind the bar. "This had better be good, Roger. I assume we have a problem."

Bowtie man turned around and the colour drained from his face.

*

Two thousand miles away, another day in paradise was unfolding. Sid was reading. Dave was leching at pretty girls in and half out of swimsuits and Tom was sleeping restlessly. Tom had travelled back in time to the day he had met his future wife. They were sat in the unassuming canteen of the local hospital. Tom was in his new white coat. Stethoscope hanging dangerously from his pocket, and the cardiac arrest bleep on the table, next to his chilli, chips and beans. The surviving residue from the metal containers behind the counter. He looked at the girl sat alone at the corner of the room. She was studiously ignoring him. Her white coat was more tired than his. The pockets more frayed.

He walked over. "Can I join you?"

"No. This table is reserved for Senior House Officers," she replied.

"Oh," he said. "Sorry," and walked back. She continued to eat silently from her plate, consisting entirely of chips and ketchup. He returned to his table and sat down again. The microwave alarmed to signal more fine cuisine was successfully incinerated behind the hotplate, as Tom leapt up from his seat and then sat down again in embarrassment. The girl in the corner managed the first smile of her lunch break.

"No defibrillator will revive that food," she informed the startled looking junior houseman. "A semitone higher for the arrest bleep," she added. "You'll soon learn."

"Oh, um, thanks," he stumbled.

"And stick to the chips. Your bowels will thank you." Her own bleep sounded, at which point she stood up, gathered her belongings, and walked gracefully out of the canteen without looking back. He was a mix of furious, embarrassed, and bewitched. She had nice legs too... In the next instant, the scene shifted, and she came back into the canteen twenty years older. "Are you coming back or what?" she asked. "I'm not waiting for you if you don't."

He tried to call out to her but couldn't utter a word. He tried to get up, but his legs wouldn't move.

"Your choice," she said. "Don't blame me when this dies." She threw the arrest bleep at him. "All you ever answer to." And then she'd turned and disappeared into the distance. He knew she wouldn't come back. He felt overwhelmed and defeated.

Tom was suddenly awoken by a splash of water on his side. It was Ann and Diego.

"Tom, you sleep more than my old cat. Come on in."

"Old Silvester here is protecting his ninth life," replied Dave with a grin. "I'll join you instead. I'm far better looking."

"Be careful you don't drown Tweetie Pie then," Ann quipped back at him as she looked up at his shorts.

"Who is Tweetie Pie?" asked Diego.

"Tweetie Pie is a heroic canary from a kid's cartoon," retorted Dave, defensively.

"Tweetie Pie is an annoying twat who teases the cat who wants to kill him. Very appropriate under the current circumstances," Tom added with a wry smile.

Tom got up, splashed them back, called over to Sid and cautiously sank into the water. He had awoken with a heavy feeling in his stomach. He had loved the girl in the canteen dearly. They married within eight months after she had become pregnant and stayed together for twenty more years, but his career ruined any chances of their relationship succeeding. Now the cold water distracted him, and he stopped for a moment to feel the heat of the sun on his face. The water running off his head had disguised the few tears that had escaped earlier from his eyes. The alcohol cravings had almost completely settled now, and he had poured the last of the rum into the pool drain without telling Sid.

"Bollocks," he said to himself. "New start, here I come." A volleyball skimmed the side of his head. "You're such a child, Dave," he said and turned around to find an apologetic Sid grinning back at him.

"So sorry, I can't throw straight." And he winked.

Tom smiled. New beginnings for all.

*

Five miles away, a pale, slim, raven-haired woman boarded a bus from the airport. She had a vague idea where she was going. She had caught a last-minute flight from Stansted airport and was wearing the same clothes she had slept in earlier on the plane. Her luggage consisted of a plastic bag and a rucksack, which contained most of her worldly possessions of any value, including her passport, her diary, and her phone. A bus pulled up at the stop, belching blue smoke, and she showed the postcard to the bus driver with a weak smile and pointed at the hotel name. He smiled back.

"Ah, new life. *Moy Bien*. I tell you when you stop." She wondered how he'd guessed she was British, but Eloy, the driver, had seen many things on his bus over the years. And this girl was escaping something. The distinctive green Harrods carrier bag was a clue.

She looked tired and sad. He couldn't read the tattoo on her arm, but he guessed that it was something more profound than worn by the usual holidaymaker. He also noticed her few possessions, her leather jacket and the black trainers that didn't match her outfit. She was striking but somewhat unkempt. As she sat down on the bus, she carefully took the beige folder out of the plastic bag. She put it in the rucksack and took out a small bottle of water. A dry blast of heat had engulfed her as soon as she had stepped out of the aircraft, along with a clean smell, a mix of herbs and pine needles. She hadn't been able to place it, but it was strangely comforting and familiar. A clatter of insect noise had whined and clicked somewhere in the distance. She took a gulp of water.

"You very hot," said the driver. She shot him a suspicious look. "You need cream for sun here or very bad." He pointed upwards. "Very hot." But he seemed genuinely concerned. He pointed to a discarded half bottle of sunscreen in the bin. "Many euros," he said. "They no take back England on airplane. Please take." She spotted a phone charger lead in the same bin. "Please take," he said imploringly.

As they drove, she was aware of him glancing furtively at her in the mirror. And yet it wasn't with the usual grubby lustful looks that met her as she worked in the pub. She couldn't quite place it. Finally, after twenty minutes, he showed her where to get off the bus and pointed to a building. She thanked him gracefully.

"*Gracias,*" she said. It was one of only two Spanish words that she knew.

"*De nada,*" he replied.

He had given her some sweets to take with her. They were green and yellow, but she was hungry, and they smelled sweet. She crunched three in one go and felt the rush of the sugar hit a few moments later.

"*Eres guapísima,*" he whispered quietly after her retreating figure, as a tear fell onto his cheek. She reminded him so much of his only daughter who had left the island years many earlier for a better life, and never returned. "*Dios te bendiga*".

Perhaps all men weren't the same after all.

CHAPTER SIX: THE KINDNESS OF STRANGERS

Lexy wasn't quite sure what to expect when she arrived. She hadn't booked a room. They had no idea she was coming. They might even have left the island by now. She went to the reception desk, but no one was there. She was hot and sweaty. Beads of perspiration ran down her forehead and back. She needed a shower and the toilet. She needed a drink. Suddenly she felt lightheaded. She sat down and the room began to spin. She put her head between her knees and closed her eyes tightly. A few moments seemed to pass.

"*Señorita. Estas bien?*" It was an elderly lady. A cleaner from the complex. She had a wise, sun-baked face with small brown eyes and a blue uniform with an apron. Lexy looked up. She had been asleep. She sat up with a start and found, to her relief, her rucksack, and the carrier bag untouched by her side. She looked at the lady. Her bladder ached.

"Come," said the woman and gently beckoned her over.

She showed her a small bedroom with a toilet and a shower. The bed was freshly made up. "Please" she said and gave Lexy soap and a towel from a pile on her trolley. Then she gave her a bottle of water and a biscuit and with a shushing voice, placed her finger to her lips. Her face beamed. "No one stay here today."

It was another simple act of kindness from a complete stranger. Lexy attempted a smile back and reached for her purse, but the elderly woman made a dismissive gesture and smiled again.

"Sleep," she said. "Go sleep. I wake you when I finish."

Lexy could have cried with relief. The cleaning lady had even left her with some shampoo, shower gel and deodorant. After a long, refreshing shower, she crawled under the sheets and fell asleep within a minute. And she dreamt. Not peaceful holiday dreams, but of the pub, of yellow Bob and the bowtie man, who were now all driving a bus directly towards her. She was awoken by a gentle knock at the door. It was the cleaning lady.

"*Ola*, so sorry. Must clean room."

And so Lexy got up, collected her few things, and left. She hugged the lady as she left. "*Gracias,*" she said quietly.

The lady hugged her back. "De nada, niñita. Dios te bendiga."

Lexy walked through the hotel and out into the pool area, not quite sure what to expect. She could hardly ask for the three amigos at the reception desk. She stood for a moment, and then she heard them before she saw them.

"Throw it here, come on." Laughter followed. "Sorry can we have our ball back? Sid, you're crap at throwing." More laughter followed, along with splashing noises. And then, words that for once delighted her, rather than irritated.

"Bugger me. We'll finally get a decent beer around here! Sid, you'd better stay in the water." More laughter. Tom climbed out of the pool to greet her. Sid stood in the pool with his mouth wide open.

"You made it!" announced Tom with delight, and he hugged her, half soaking her in the process.

"It was the detailed instructions on the postcard," laughed Lexy. "And it's Lexy, please. I'm not a barmaid anymore. I resigned yesterday."

"Come in the pool," said Dave, "the water's really wet."

"No swimsuit," said Lexy. She ignored the facial expression that followed.

Sid had finally found his voice. "Lexy, it's wonderful that you came. Can I get you a hot drink or something? Are you alright?" He started to get out of the pool. Lexy smiled.

"That would be nice, actually. Do you have a charger too?"

"Your knight, Sir Sid, has a large white one," laughed Dave.

Meanwhile, two nearby sunbathers in bikinis were watching the scene with a mix of emotions.

"Ladies," announced Tom, "meet Lexy. Lexy is the latest recruit for the Atlantic Oceans Seven!"

Lexy looked bemused.

"She's our Julia Roberts."

Sid beamed. Rhiannon frowned a little. Tom smiled, sensing the slight tension developing in the air.

"And Lexy, please meet the two loveliest reps on the island. Ann and Rhiannon. Our saviours here in the sun."

Rhiannon managed a smile. Ann hugged Lexy.

"How lovely to meet you. Come with me, and you can borrow one of my costumes." She reached out to take her hand.

"Do you have a room?" asked Sid.

"Down boy!" replied Dave.

"No, I mean if she doesn't, she can have mine, and I'll share with you or Tom."

"Tom will be delighted to share with you," said Dave, who sensed a fresh opportunity with Rhiannon, and didn't want a roommate unless it was female and preferably recently spurned.

"Lexy can share with us," said Rhiannon quickly. "We have plenty of room."

Dave's face dropped visibly. Thirty minutes later, Lexy emerged in a simple white bikini with a towel wrapped around her waist. She was clearly self-conscious, and Rhiannon was pleased to note that she hadn't shaved her legs. She had a lithe figure, though, and a number of tattoos in addition to the one on her arm. A panther covered her left shoulder blade, and a dragon ran along the length of her spine. The crudely tattooed lettering of the word 'Lexy' was covered by the towel. She was clearly embarrassed to show this. A number of small round scars were also visible. She told people that these were from a chickenpox infection, but they were actually punishment from her biological father's Embassy cigarettes when she was too young to fight back. Sid gazed at her as if she were the loveliest thing he had ever seen. He mouthed the word 'gosh'. Lexy looked back at him. And suddenly, she felt beautiful for the first time in her life. He had put his shirt back on, and now went to the bar area, coming back a few minutes later with a precariously balanced pot of tea, cup, some biscuits, and a small bowl of mixed nuts.

"I hope it's ok," he said. "Would you like something else to eat? A cake or some chocolate or...?"

She looked at Sid. His kind, timid eyes briefly met hers. And then quite unexpectedly, she reached forward and kissed him gently on the cheek. "You are lovely," she said. It was the briefest of brushes of lips against skin. This was followed by a brief but awed silence amongst the group of friends, broken eventually by Dave.

"You do realise that Sid will now never wash his face

again!" The comment broke the spell and laughter followed.

"He's a gentleman, that's all" said Lexy, but she blushed. Possibly for only the second time in her life. "Thank you, Sid." Sid simply stood still. Looking astonished.

"Um, you're very welcome," he eventually stammered. And, finally, he beamed. The face was now that of a much younger man. He had changed surprisingly little since leaving his heart behind in Kerala many years earlier... "Oh my gosh," he added. "I think I may need to sit down."

CHAPTER SEVEN: HIPS AND TRICKS

The evening had been a blur. Tom, still on the soft drinks, but a changed man, was relaxed, funny and visibly looking healthier. Lexy was wearing new clothes, which Sid had insisted on paying for, whilst adding, "I hope you don't think I'm being inappropriate".

He had sent Rhiannon and Ann out with her, clutching his credit card. She looked fresh, clean and... Sid had to admit, absolutely breath-taking. She was wearing a white summer dress, tied at the waist and with a lace-like pattern around the bodice section and long skirt. Her legs were bare but now clean-shaven, and her hair was shiny and loose around her shoulders. She still wore her black leather jacket and smelt subtly of expensive fragrance. She insisted on wearing her trainers, but oddly, they matched the outfit. Both Dave and Tom had stared open-mouthed when she had first entered the bar.

"Bloody hell..." Dave had said, simply. "You scrub up!"

Not to be outdone. Rhiannon and Ann were also looking lovely, Ann in simple but tight white jeans and a bright yellow blouse and Rhiannon in an orange dress with a plunging neckline, highlighting her even tan.

Dave, Tom, and Sid looked at each other. Tom still in his Dr. Martens and tired jeans, Sid in black polyester work trousers and a fraying white shirt and Dave... well, Dave, of course, was wearing white jeans, an open denim shirt and canvas shoes.

"I'm taking you two clothes shopping tomorrow," he'd said to Sid and Tom.

"You bloody well are not." Ann shot back. "We are. And we'll knock years off all three of you old duffers."

Dave looked slightly hurt.

"Oh Dave, I bet you even still wear Brut 55 aftershave," laughed Ann.

"Like my grandad," added Rhiannon.

Dave grimaced slightly. "Hate the stuff," he said casually, whilst mentally making a note to pour it down the sink as soon as he got back to his room. Sid had quietly watched. It was the white dress that had mesmerised him and stimulated the memories of Kerala to flood back from so many years ago. The last time they had seen each other. Priya had worn a very similar one that day. A soft touch of a hand brought him back into the present.

"Good evening, Dr Sid," she said and smiled.

"My goodness, you look... such a lady," he replied, his mouth gaping involuntarily. Lexy stood by his side.

"Get a room, you two!" laughed Dave. The moment abruptly ended and was followed rapidly by laughter, pizzas, plates of olives and large bowls of fresh salad. Diego had joined them and brought his guitar. They sang along to him later, badly but enthusiastically. Later, Ann and Rhiannon had taken them all to the local karaoke bar, where Dave, Tom and Sid had sung their own version of the old 'Moon River' classic, with Dave pretending to moon at Rhiannon at the appropriate points in the song.

"Not quite as originally sung by Andy Williams," announced Tom as they all sat down.

"Audrey Hepburn actually," said Lexy.

"Breakfast at Tiffany's," smiled Sid as he looked at her.

"Beautiful film. So romantic," he added wistfully. She blushed imperceptibly this time but smiled. Tom beamed and put his arms around his two friends. Not even a milligram of alcohol had passed his lips, and yet he felt happily drunk. Thirty years seemed to have lifted from his face within a few days. They'd all agreed to meet up again by the pool the following morning, but before they'd parted for the night, Lexy had taken Tom to one side, as the others were still chatting and joking with each other.

"I think we need to talk," she said.

"Sid is married if that's what you're asking," said Tom.

"No, no, I didn't mean that." A flicker of irritation crossed her face. Was he?

"I've found something, and I think it could be important. It affects the three of you. It was something left in my pub back in London."

She paused momentarily. Astonishingly, she did slightly miss The Wolf and Whistle. In a strange way, she even missed old yellow Bob. She wondered if he'd managed to add a few further shades of yellow to his complexion since she'd last seen him. They'd occasionally had karaoke at that pub too, but usually delivered by the tone-deaf to the tone-deaf.

"Ok, let's all meet up for lunch at the pool bar, around twelve," he replied.

"No, I think we're going to need somewhere where we can't be overhead," she'd suggested. "Let's meet later in the afternoon. Just the four of us."

"Ok, I'll ask Diego if he knows somewhere."

And then Sid and Dave had pulled him back onto the stage for an encore.

"Sorry Miss Lexy, we need someone who can sing," Dave had laughed.

This time, they all sang the 'Ying Tong' song by The Goons. It had been Tom's father's favourite and it was the only other song he knew all the lyrics to. The mixed crowd, mostly comprised of drunken British holidaymakers and Spanish bar staff, loved it! It was raucous, silly, and required a delightful burst of high- pitched, porky pig type squeaking when the heroes of the ditty are tragically blasted by a falling bomb. The night had ended with hot chocolate and doughnuts at a small bar that Diego had taken them to. Ann and Diego had left together. Sid and Lexy had bid their mutual goodnights like a pair of infatuated teenagers following what seemed like a long, intimate conversation. And an even odder thing had happened. Dave had not made his customary, clumsy, and expected, pass at Rhiannon. Instead, he had kissed her on the hand and said goodnight. And for once, he had seemed tongue-tied and awkward.

"Oh, bollocks," he'd mumbled to himself. "I don't fucking believe it. At bloody fifty."

"All ok?" Tom had asked.

"Nothing. Um. Too many of those, um, olives, no doubt," he'd replied. "Bet I get the shits later. Ha, ha! Serve me right eh?!"

His stomach continued to churn, but this didn't feel like gastroenteritis. Sid thought he knew the ailment that was affecting Dave's stomach too. Creating the abdominal peristalsis effect, accompanied by a slight tachycardia, erythema of the cheeks and intermittent dysphasia. It was clearly contagious. He felt exactly the same about Lexy.

*

It was a Saturday morning in May 1992. In a West Yorkshire hospital, Tom, wearing traditional theatre blues, was trailing around the orthopaedic ward. A long weekend ahead on call beckoned. "Bollocks" he chunnered to himself. His little boy would be missing him. Aged almost two, he was currently Tom's biggest fan, largely as a result of him being able to convert the hysterical child into a squealing, giggling heap by simply swinging him over his neck and dangling him by the feet. Aided by the opposite but amusing effect this had on the child's mother.

"You'll bloody drop him one day, then you won't be laughing," she'd always scold him. He never did.

"I'm so sorry, I hope you don't mind me shadowing you," the medical student had said by his side, breaking his reverie. She was young, pretty, and still full of enthusiasm for medicine. She looked school-aged. By contrast, Tom was weary, aging by the day and chronically sleep deprived.

"It's not you," said Tom. "Sorry, I'm just knackered. Let's crack on."

"Sister, please can I do a pre-anaesthetic check on the old boy needing the hip." Edgar was eighty-five. He had a fairly thin medical file and had broken his hip the previous morning after falling off a stepladder. Saturday was the mop-up day. Tom had been working as a trainee Anaesthetist at the hospital for nearly ten months now. He was officially allowed to gas, IV or spinal block anyone from the age of three up to one hundred on his own. He had become pretty competent, largely thanks to the teaching from the consultants in the unit, who ranged in personality from the very cautious to the outright cavalier in their approach to the specialty.

Dr Bob was his favourite. Tom wasn't quite sure if he was extremely clever, barking mad, or both. Bob was a great but hidden comic, with an acerbic wit combined with a perfectly timed, deadpan delivery. He had managed to convince Tom of a chronic condition called 'PPD', which he said his matronly senior female colleague was, alas, severely afflicted by. Poor thing, said Bob. It affects her mood, energy levels and general circulation. She needs regular pelvic injections, but no one will give her them.

When it turned out that PPD stood for Pelvic Protein Deficiency and wasn't in the International Classification of Diseases, the penny had finally dropped. Tom's obvious look of concern for her wellbeing had entertained the ODAs for weeks. He apparently had named his children after items of medical equipment. Imogen being named after the Image Intensifier in theatre, Haley after the anaesthetic gas halothane and his latest, Emery, from the newest type of body scanner of the time.

He punned the name of drugs. The sedating anti-sickness medication droperidol had morphed into drop-deaderol, owing to its unfortunate occasional permanent side-effect on patients in the intensive care unit. The intensive care unit was renamed 'expensive care', Groperol was his nickname for the drug propofol, mainly due to its occasional effect of causing explicit sexual dreams in patients during anaesthesia followed by brief but hilarious carnal demands on the recovery staff during the immediate post-operative period.

Vomitil (stemetil) was for nausea prevention. "Could I have some sucks please?" he'd ask when he wanted the (usually female) assistant to pass him the vial of muscle relaxant suxamethonium - always delivered with the same expression of virginal innocence. He also occasionally sabotaged the anaesthetic machine for unwitting trainees mid-surgery to check that they could find the disconnection quickly. "Good practice for emergencies," he'd say afterwards to the sweaty, hyperventilating victim - hopefully only the doctor.

Tom always carried the crash bleep to assist at cardiac arrests in the hospital but couldn't answer it whilst in the operating theatre. Nine o'clock to one o'clock was the worst time to decide to collapse on a Saturday. Yes, Tom felt fairly confident that today's hip operation would be finished within an hour or so. It was a good opportunity to try out another spinal anaesthetic too. This was the technique whereby a needle, barely thicker than a human hair, could be inserted between the posterior vertebral processes in the lower back, enabling the injection of a local anaesthetic agent to create numbness below the waist and thereby minimise any additional painkillers needed during the operation. Much safer for older patients in particular.

"How long will it last for?" asked the student.

"A couple of hours at least," replied Tom. "That's plenty of time for a routine hip."

"What if it takes longer?" she'd asked.

"Our surgeon today, Terry, is the quickest hip fixer I know." And he'll be on a promise at lunchtime too, no doubt, he thought to himself.

The medical student smiled pleasantly. "Gosh, this is so interesting," she said. "How many operations do we have today?"

"Four," replied Tom. "We should be done by one. I'm covering this list, the reg is covering maternity. And the consultant is down at the goldmine in case we need him." (Dr Bob's name for the local private hospital).

Edgar was a pleasant man. "Bit of trouble with the old ticker, but not bad for me age otherwise," he had said to Tom when asked about his health. Tom had skimmed through the thin records and was satisfied that there wasn't much else of note in them. He clearly avoided doctors. That was probably why he was still alive at eighty-five.

"Routine group and save, an FBC and U&Es, should be ok here," he said to the student. "The clerking- in doc will have done those yesterday. Can you double- check?"

"Oh, yes," replied the student. She didn't want to seem ignorant, but she had no idea what he was talking about. She'd look it up.

Forty-five minutes later, they were in the anaesthetic room. Old Edgar had opted for the headphones during surgery. "I don't want to hear the sawing noise," he said to Tom. "I used to work in a wood mill."

To Tom's relief, the spinal needle slipped easily between the old bones in Edgar's spine, despite its slightly misshapen appearance, with the eager student watching every move. Edgar was soon numb enough to go into theatre to begin his surgical adventure. The staff were jovial enough. Terry, the surgeon, looked hungover but otherwise seemed in a good mood. He was about to launch into a description of his antics of the night before when Tom abruptly turned up the volume on the headset.

"I'm not bloody deaf," the old boy had replied with indignation.

"He'll soon wish he was," quipped Terry, just out of earshot.

Soon peace had returned to the theatre. Tom was sat reading the morning paper at the draped head of the bed, and Edgar was snoring softly. The whirr of a bone saw or drill occasionally punctuated the air. The monitors winked at each other alternately. It was a contented Saturday morning scene, interspersed with the occasional frying aroma of tissue being cauterised. Every now and then, the student would ask a question, and Tom would politely reply before returning to his *Guardian*.

"You still a fookin' lefty?" jeered Terry, peering across the drapes. "On your salary, you'll soon change your mind! Good job some of us can do some real graft."

"Orthopaedics is a good medical speciality to consider, as you only need an O-Level in woodwork," Tom informed the medical student at his side loudly. "It's also good rehabilitation for rugby players who've had head injuries."

There was laughter, and he dodged the swab that was lobbed at him by the surgeon. Terry was an amiable sort. He'd never managed to pass his higher orthopaedic exams, but they'd given him a job as a permanent middle-grade doctor, which meant he ended up doing most of his consultant's work for him. He was also a cracking surgeon. Tom liked working with him, and they drank beer together intermittently. He had five children and was built like a prop forward. Another half hour passed.

Tom had read most of the paper when he felt a damp sensation on his foot. He looked down. A puddle of blood was developing on the floor under Edgar's hip.

"Everything ok down there, Terry?" asked Tom. Terry had been uncharacteristically quiet for the last fifteen minutes or so. Tom could see beads of perspiration on his forehead.

"Being a bit of a fucker, this hip," Terry grunted back. "The bones are soft, and he bleeds like a stuck pig every time I saw the bone."

Alarm suddenly struck Tom. "How much blood has he lost, Terry?"

"Couple of pints at least," said Terry. "It's going to take a while longer yet too."

Tom looked at Edgar. At the slightly bossed forehead. He remembered the oddly-shaped spine. "Oh, holy fuck," he said to himself quietly. "Edgar could have Paget's Disease." A condition causing softening of the bones. And a tendency for them to both break and bleed more easily.

"Could you ask blood bank to send us a couple of units of blood please?" he asked the ODA, with an air of calm. "Theatre two. Soon as."

"Yes boss," said Clive, his ever calm, ever-patient assistant.

A few minutes passed. "Boss, a quick word?" said Clive. He spoke quietly. "They haven't got a group and save sample for him in the lab. Shall I take one now?"

"Shit. I mean, yes please. Didn't the fucking SHO do it yesterday? Typical. The only time we actually need it!"

"Is everything ok?" asked the medical student with interest.

"Yes," Clive and Tom replied in unison. It clearly wasn't.

Clive rummaged under the surgical drapes and took a blood sample from Edgar's arm. Thirty minutes later, Tom was still anxiously awaiting the blood to arrive as Edgar's blood pressure was beginning to dip.

"Feel a bit dizzy doc," said Edgar. "My chest hurts too." He pointed helpfully to his chest, dislodging one of the drapes.

Tom was now sweating properly. He'd given the old man a couple of bags of fluid already and was aware that the thinner his blood became, the more the hip would bleed. He gave him two puffs of an Angina spray for good measure.

"You'll be fine, Edgar," he said. Edgar felt reassured. That was nice. Edgar shouldn't have felt reassured.

Tom's pager sounded. *CARDIAC ARREST, WARD 8. CARDIAC ARREST WARD 8.* They'd have to manage without him.

"Clive, can you tell the reg we need some help here?"

"She's in theatre already, Tom. Emergency section. Cord prolapse, They're all tied up. Literally."

"Shit. Can you call Bob?"

"He'll be down the goldmine, Tom, you know that."

Tom hesitated momentarily. "Bollocks. Just leave him a message. We're not going to get this list done. There's an appendix, too on a kid. I'm supposed to be doing a round on expensive care this afternoon too."

For the first time in his career as an anaesthetist, Tom was now well and truly ruffled. Meanwhile, the puddle at his feet was becoming a lake. At least the spare blood had arrived from transfusion. One bag was being physically squeezed through Edgar's fragile veins by Clive, and the other was resting in the cleavage of one of the better-endowed theatre nurses to get to body temperature.

"You bloody owe me," she'd said to Clive with a wink. Terry had also noticed.

"This is so interesting," said the medical student. "I've never seen this sort of thing before."

Neither have I, Tom thought to himself. He was distracted by a sudden noise from Edgar.

"Ow! I think I felt something then doc." Tom looked at the clock. Two hours had passed since the start of the operation. Shit. The spinal was wearing off.

"Terry, you're going to have to stop for a minute," said Tom. "I need to turn him on his back so we can put him to sleep for a bit."

"You'll be fucking lucky," said Terry. "His legs in three clamps, mate. I daren't move him."

Tom looked in alarm at Edgar. He was looking grey. His pulse rate had climbed. His blood pressure was falling.

"Tell transfusion we need four more units," said Tom. "And Clive, we're going to have to tube him on the table."

"If he vomits," said Clive, "we can't turn him."

"Can you get Bob on the phone then?"

"You'll be lucky, he's flat out down the goldmine today. They've got some problem down there too."

The cardiac arrest call went out again. This time it was in casualty. "Bollocks, bollocks, bollocks," muttered Tom to himself. The new Spanish house officer would be on her own down there. She couldn't cannulate a vein to save her life.

"Clive, is there a spare ODA we can send down to Cas to give them a hand?" He knew from the look he got back, that there wasn't. Hope it's not a kid, he thought to himself.

Tom thought quickly. "Clive, how about a Larry? Could we vent him on that?"

A Larry, properly known as a laryngeal mask airway and improperly known as a fanny-on-a-stick, (owing to its astonishing similarity in appearance to the female external genitalia) was still a relatively new item of equipment, normally only used for very brief anaesthetics, and certainly not for venting (ventilating) patients. There was a significant risk if the patient vomited during the procedure of developing fatal aspiration pneumonia. Not a good option for a frail eighty-five-year-old.

"Are you asking me, should we or could we?" asked Clive. He ushered Tom out of earshot from the rest of the staff. "You'll have to sedate him heavily, so he doesn't feel anything, and if you do, he'll stop breathing by himself. Even Bob doesn't vent on a fanny."

"Any brighter ideas?"

"Nope. I'll get one."

"Better not call it that in front of the student Clive," said Tom with an attempt at a smile.

"Roger," said Clive.

"Beth actually," said Tom.

"I'll go get the next pint of blood from our resident blood warmer," said Clive.

"You bloody won't," said Doris, the resident blood warmer. "Cheeky sod!" She carefully passed Clive the bag at almost perfect body temperature.

Another half an hour passed. Somehow, Clive and Tom between them managed to sedate Edgar, not lethally drop his blood pressure, place (very carefully) and inflate (even more carefully) the laryngeal mask airway adjacent to Edgar's voice box and gently hand ventilate him for the last fifteen minutes. Tom watched the monitors like a hawk. Cold sweat drenched his theatre blues. His white theatre shoes were now burgundy. Terry's boss had also joined him at the working end.

"Were you trained by a fucking tree surgeon?" he boomed (rather unkindly under the circumstances) after inspecting the remnants of Edgar's hip.

"No, you did sir..." Terry immediately regretted his honesty.

"We think he may have undiagnosed Paget's of the bone. Not Terry's fault," added Tom lamely in support. "Softens the bones and they tend to bleed a lot..." he added, unnecessarily. Terry's boss seemed unmoved. He cursed intermittently, barked orders at the staff, and made a lot of drilling and hammering noises. Tom dreaded to think what remnants of Edgar's original hip joint remained intact. Another hour passed, and finally, the wound clips were being applied.

"Is he still alive?" Terry asked anxiously when his consultant had finally stormed out again (back to the goldmine whence he came). Four hours, four pints of blood, three litres of intravenous fluids, some frusemide had passed. In addition to a lot of propofol, a fair amount of morphine had been used. Theatre two looked like a scene from The Texas Chainsaw Massacre.

"Of course," replied Clive. "But his CD player isn't so lucky. It also looks like he may have a slightly shorter leg on one side. And he's been dreaming of Doris's tits for the last hour."

Doris smiled and gave a little curtsy.

There was laughter. Of relief. Of the disaster that had nearly unfolded in front of them all. And for which Tom felt largely responsible. The expensive care unit was awaiting its latest recruit. Bob had briefly popped back from the goldmine for the child needing the appendicectomy. The reg had done the ward round, and the final two cases of the morning had been delayed until they'd had a chance to clean theatre and eat something. The student looked at Tom brightly.

"Gosh, that was so interesting. I think I may want to do

anaesthetics. Can I join you for the afternoon list?"

Tom, sodden with sweat, clammy, grey, and thinking he may be starting to hallucinate, had no words. He was fairly certain that his patient wouldn't be testing his new hip out either. In the background, the crash bleep sounded impatiently once again.

*

It was Sunday morning. The rest of the day had passed relatively uneventfully. He'd slept for most of the night too. He had some new theatre shoes that were no longer in LMS livery. He paused at the door of the intensive care unit and crossed his fingers. Edgar had taken a long time to wake up the previous day. Tom looked at the six- bedded unit. He recognised the first five patients from previously. The sixth bed was clean and had crisp sheets folded on it.

Tom's heart sank. Oh god, I've killed him, he thought.

Meanwhile, Dr Bob came around the corner. "Are you looking for Mr E?" he asked pleasantly. "Slightly unconventional anaesthetic, I hear?"

"Um, yes," said Tom.

"You'd better go to ward four. He's furious with you."

"He can speak? He's not dead? No brain damage? No heart failure?" blurted out Tom.

"He can certainly speak," replied Bob. "Mostly in tongues initially, but I believe he thinks you broke his CD player." Bob smiled. "Good effort yesterday," he said kindly. "Most people would have panicked. Venting on a fanny eh…? Must try it." And with those words of wisdom, he swept out of the ward.

"He comes from a planet many light-years from ours," said the ICU sister with a smile. "Go see Edgar, Tom. And maybe have another shower?"

CHAPTER EIGHT: RESTORATION AND REVELATION

Right," the three girls had said. Sid, Dave, and Tom were ordered to have haircuts. Diego knew a Turkish barber nearby. He winked conspiratorially at Ann.

"You will not know your friends after this," he said.

"Are we going to be brainwashed?" asked Dave innocently.

"Your brain need very big wash," said Diego with a smile. They all laughed.

"You look like old man," the Turkish barber had said to Sid. "When I finish, you look like son!" The first decent haircut since his wedding thirty years previously, along with some dark hair dye, applied to the greyer areas, had had the most startling effect on Sid.

"Your glasses. They shit," said Hasim, the head barber. "My friend is good eye man. He get you contact lenses. One hour. Give me glasses. You see through these bottle tops?"

"I think he means bottle bottoms," added Tom helpfully.

Sid obediently handed over his glasses but looked anxious. "Yes. My prescription hasn't changed much…" He could now see very little at all. The glasses were gone.

"Does Jack Duckworth come here?" asked Dave.

"If, did, he not have shit glasses," replied Hasim.

Meanwhile, Dave was soon receiving the attention of Yusuf, who had a terrifying-looking cutthroat razor in one hand and a lather brush in the other.

"I try not to sneeze too bad," said Yusuf with a grin. "You like meat pies? If I sneeze really bad, I make you a girl." Dave sat very, very still for the next ten minutes, which seemed much longer. Tom was in the midst of the Turkish version of a head massage. It was rough, but amazingly therapeutic.

"You worry much," said the brusque elderly man, with spindly arms but who had clearly eaten his spinach that morning.

"I worry that you'll break my skull," winced Tom in reply.

The old man laughed. "I only break neck once. And he much older than you."

Tom failed to relax further. Finally, all three stood up to leave. The result was nothing short of miraculous. Twenty euros each had removed approximately a year per euro from all three of them. Yusuf gave Dave a little wave as he left. Dave looked a combination of alarmed and slightly flattered. An hour and a half had passed, three clean-shaven and barely recognisable men returned. The biggest change was for Sid who was also wearing his new contact lenses. They were soft lenses, and surprisingly comfortable, though he did feel slightly disorientated in them and kept blinking.

"You see my friend again in week," Hasim had said. "He check you no go blind!" He had slapped Sid affectionately on the back. The biggest change in Sid was his face. The Dennis

Healey eyebrows had been replaced by elegant, defining dark lines. Along with his nostril and ear hair, which had disappeared without trace.

"You handsome old bugger you," said Dave. "Lexy's going to jump you before you get out of the changing room…" He saw the wince in Sid's face and instantly regretted his crass remark. "Sorry, mate. I just mean you must have been a bit neglected over the years. I had an old Triumph Spitfire once…"

"Quiet time Dave," added Tom. "Diplomat training starts again on Monday."

Sid was quiet for a few minutes as they walked back to the agreed meeting place. "I was considered handsome once," he said. "The girls in the village used to flutter their eyelashes at me or giggle and run away."

"Why did you move to England then?" asked Tom.

Sid looked down for a moment. "It's a long story," he said.

"Did it involve a girl?" asked Tom gently.

"Yes," replied Sid. "A forbidden romance." He went quiet again.

"Perhaps you'll meet her again?" asked Tom.

Sid quietly shook his head. "Gosh these contact lenses feel strange," he said, quickly changing the subject.

"Your eyes look fucking huge!" exclaimed Dave.

"Dave means that they suit you," said Tom. "In his Australian cultural attaché sort of way."

Sid looked puzzled. "Is Dave part Australian?"

Tom and Dave both roared with laughter and all three relaxed once again.

"Sid, you are the Ernie Wise to Eric Morecambe," said Dave.

"It's a compliment, I think," said Tom. "He means you're funny and underrated. Eric wouldn't be so funny without Ernie, and vice versa."

"Maybe, Dave, you are Stan Laurel," replied Sid with a grin. They all laughed again.

"I used to be considered funny once too," smiled Sid.

"You're in comedy school now, Sid," beamed Tom back. For the first time in two years, Tom could move his neck to both sides without getting pain down his back. For effect, Sid, Tom and Dave decided to walk past the girls to see if they'd notice the difference. On the second walk past, Ann gave out a little squeal when she saw them.

"What the f...?" she mouthed. Dave looked smart, Tom rejuvenated and Sid. Well Sid was beyond recognition. Lexy looked at Sid.

"Where are your glasses?" she asked after a moment's pause. "You look so... different. I can see your eyes... god, where are your eyebrows...?"

"The glasses are currently being recycled," said Dave.

"Into champagne bottles," added Sid with a self-effacing grin.

"And his eyebrows have been donated to the Alopecia Unit," added Tom.

Lexy was struggling to reply.

"Maybe we can all have a glass of champagne after we finish shopping then!" added Rhiannon with a smile. She followed this with something in Welsh to Ann, who snorted back in laughter.

"Not on my island!" replied Diego, who had been quietly observing the six of them. "This is *Espana*. We drink Cava here!" He raised a dramatic arm in toast. Rhiannon looked relieved that none of the others spoke Welsh. Or so she thought. Sid's face twitched momentarily. He smiled at Dave but said nothing. Next, they were taken to the shops. Not the tourist ones, nor one of the smart, air conditioned boutiques. They headed past the market. In one corner, a small sign announced a shop marked 'men's tailor'. Underneath in neat handwriting were the words, 'Best price. No rubbish. Fit your size.'

"My goodness," said Dave. "Is this a lesser-known branch of Harrods? Maybe Horrids?"

They all laughed, except Diego. He said something quickly in Spanish to the tailor, who grinned in return and nodded in agreement.

"He says you have one hundred euros each maximum to woo these beautiful ladies." Diego frowned. "Except this one!" The tailor pointed to Ann hastily. "She is already wooed."

"Woo woo!" replied Dave.

Suddenly a tape measure was brought out. The tailor laughed as Dave breathed in. "You can have smaller size, or you can breathe. Oxygen is better, my friend."

He measured all three of them very quickly, their collar, chest, waist, arm and inside leg measurements with deft precision, accompanied by interspersed tutting noises. Dave looked embarrassed.

"I plan to lose some off here," he patted his modest paunch. His sentence hung gently in the light breeze.

"Boy or girl?" asked the tailor pleasantly. With an affectionate extra pat. Next Tom and finally Sid.

"You go to gym, yes?" he said simply to Sid. "Maybe take your friends next time," he laughed.

"They all need something casual but smart," said Ann. "And jackets. With nice shirts. And some shorts."

The tailor looked alarmed.

"Best price," pointed Ann, with a smile.

"I'll do my best for you, my princess," smiled back the tailor, ingratiatingly. He liked Ann. Smart cookie. Meanwhile, Rhiannon was collecting an armful of shirts, ties, and trousers from around the racks.

"I don't like ties," said Sid rather quickly.

"Bet Lexy does," replied Dave, rather too quickly. She gave him a withering look.

"I'll get you one with a noose if you like," was Lexy's sharp retort.

Dave went quiet.

"They make my neck hot," added Sid. This wasn't quite true. His wife had attempted to strangle him with one during a row a number of years earlier, and he'd been too terrified to wear one since.

"You'd look sophisticated in a nice tie," said Ann, her head tilted slightly. "Maybe try one if Lexy or Rhiannon can find a nice one? We can always put it back."

Sid still looked a little anxious but nodded in reply. He blushed again, hidden by his dark skin.

"Dave, you need to dress your age," said Rhiannon.

"But I'm a burnt-out, fat, middle-aged git," Dave replied suddenly and rather forlornly. This surprised them all.

"We're both members of the same club," said Tom. "The, um," he thought for a moment "the B.o.f.m.a.g club as it's known. We have strange handshakes, bad jokes, and frontal disinhibition. It's very selective."

Tom looked over at Dave. It was the first time he had seen a crack appear in Dave's veneer. The apparent overconfidence was perhaps less genuine than it first appeared. Maybe there was a heart in there after all. He was still unsure about the brain, though. Further laughter followed, and eventually, the three amigos and their entourage emerged into the daylight.

"Back to the pool for a couple of hours then?" asked Dave brightly.

"Shoes, then pool," said Rhiannon.

Dave looked at his shoes.

"Especially you," she mock-scolded him.

She still wasn't quite sure what to make of him. There was

a bravado, certainly, but also a vulnerability that she couldn't quite fathom. Her feminine instinct screamed 'avoid,' and that may have explained why she felt attracted to him. This irritated her intensely. Dave looked at Rhiannon too. She was certainly very attractive, and she seemed partially aware of this, but like many beautiful women, found that men were almost reticent to approach her. She was genuinely witty, smart, and just the right amount of feisty. Dave was clumsy, funny, and intermittently, very charming. He had slept with more women than he could possibly count, and yet it had only left him with an emptiness once the chase was over. He felt lonely. It was palpable, and Rhiannon could sense it. And so they shopped for shoes. Simple deck- type shoes for all three of them. They were allowed some choice. And then back to the hotel and finally the pool once again.

*

Two hours were spent around the pool, and then Ann and Rhiannon left to perform rep duties in the hotel, followed by the party night out to the local tavernas for the travel company guests. Diego had hotel duties, and so Tom, Dave, Sid and Lexy were left together.

"Can we talk, gentlemen?" asked Lexy.

"Is this something we can talk about here?" asked Sid.

"No, we need somewhere quieter," she replied.

CHAPTER NINE: WOLVES IN SHEEP'S CLOTHING

The four sat in the comfier chairs at the far side of the unoccupied restaurant. Some even had arms. A waft of cool air blew overhead, aided rather ineptly by a fan, which hung at a jaunty angle from the stippled ceiling. A bare wire emerged tantalisingly from the wall.

"Modern art, Spanish style," smiled Tom. "This one is called, 'socket to me'."

"I think even I could be an electrician here," laughed Dave. "And I'm colour blind."

"And stupid," added Tom with a smile.

Sid walked over with a jug of water and four cups of black coffee. He had spilt a little on the tray from each in his short passage from the bar. The waiter looked in Sid's general direction and rolled his eyes slightly. Then with a shrug of his shoulders he continued doing nothing. Slowly.

"So!" said Tom. "To business. What have you discovered

in your travels through the dark side, Lexy?"

Lexy hesitated for a moment and then opened the bag which she had kept tight by her side since arriving in Tenerife.

"I found this," she said. "Mr Uriah Heap from the medical council was clearly looking for it... but he left it in my pub." She hesitated as she realised she had called it 'my pub' again. Sid smiled. She'd clearly read David Copperfield.

"He is 'ever so 'umble, not!" said Tom with a look of distaste. "Good name for him, though."

Only Dave looked slightly puzzled. "What is it?" he asked.

"I'm not sure," she said. "All I know is that your names are on the front of some of the files, and he was pretty keen to find it again. His sidekick was with him too. The whippet he clearly kicks frequently."

"Maybe he whips him too," added Dave with a smirk. Albeit a brief one, following another of Lexy's withering stares.

"Don't be an arse, Dave," said Tom. "Lexy has something important here."

"Carry on please, Lexy," encouraged Sid gently.

"So," she said. "I also overheard a previous conversation with a politician. I'm not sure which one, but I've seen him on the telly, and the customers always call him a wanker when he comes on."

"That could be one of about seven hundred then," said Tom brightly.

"Except the female ones," added Sid quietly. Lexy winked at him.

"Is he a minister?" asked Tom.

"Yes, I think so."

"I'll guess health," said Tom. He went on his phone for a moment, cursed at the Wi-Fi and finally showed her a picture.

"That must be an old one," snorted Lexy, "but yes, that's him."

"The Right Honourable Damon Forester, I believe," said Sid.

"Well, they got the right bit correct," said Tom. "They just missed out 'wing' and 'dis'. I can't bear him. He makes Thatcher look like a moderate."

"He's a right twat," said Dave helpfully.

"Thank you to our political correspondent," said Tom. "Though I believe you may have helped vote him into power." Dave attempted to protest, but he couldn't deny it.

"So why would the right-wing, dishonourable Demon Forester want to meet our man from the council in a dingy pub in central London?"

"Excuse me," said Lexy dangerously.

"Sorry, but it's hardly the bar at the Houses of Parliament," said Tom.

"Nor the council offices," said Sid with interest. "It's rather less... ornate. Though your pub was beautifully clean, Lexy," he added tactfully.

Lexy continued. "Mr Heap then, the one who always wears a bow tie...?"

"Officially Roger Wharton-Smith," said Tom. He grimaced again.

"Well, he was talking to his sidekick, let's call him the whippet for now. And he was clearly annoyed about something. I really don't think he likes doctors much either, from the comments he was making."

"He's not actually a fully registered medical doctor," said Sid. "He was a doctor originally, but he never finished his house jobs. Then he studied law."

Tom and Dave both looked at Sid in surprise.

"Well bugger me," said Dave.

"I'd rather not," replied Tom with a smirk.

"And he talked about the minister. And something about

honours," continued Lexy.

"Hah! I knew it! The bastard's after a knighthood," interjected Tom.

"Tom, we need to hear what Lexy has to say," said Sid. The gentlest of rebukes brought an apology from Tom.

"Sorry, Sid. Sorry ,Lexy. Please go on."

"And he had this bag with him, and then he seemed to get distracted, and he left them under the table when he left."

"May we see the files please?" asked Sid. Lexy passed them over to him.

"The thin one is mine. The slightly bigger one is Tom's. Um, Dave, I think this one is yours." Dave blushed. His was evidently thicker. There was another file marked 'confidential'. Sid assumed this was someone else's records.

"I'll get us some more coffee," said Lexy. Sid was about to get up when she laid a gentle hand on his shoulder, gesturing him to sit back down. Sid felt a tingle of electricity go down his back. "No, but thank you. This is my round. And you may need a bit of time to digest whatever's in those."

Ten minutes passed. Dave was sat very quietly. Sid looked in shocked disbelief. And Tom was practically apoplectic with fury.

"I... do... not... fucking... believe it!" he said finally. Slowly and fiercely. "Well, I do. But..." He was silent.

"What is it?" asked Lexy finally.

"It's judgement day," he said simply. "I think I need a beer."

Sid looked in concern at his friend. "No, you need your friends, Tom," he replied. "We're all going to need each other." He then turned to look at Lexy's face, which was showing the first signs of anxiety since he had met her.

"We need an inside man," said Dave from the corner.

"No, I think we may need an inside woman," replied Sid.

*

They'd moved back to the pool area, and Lexy was now lying on a sunbed, reading a book. Dave looked up. "*Fifty Shades?*"

"Sort of," she replied. Dave quickly shut up and lay down on his own bed. Lexy continued reading her book. Sid could see the title on its spine, and he smiled to himself. *Pride and Prejudice.* Meanwhile, Tom was in the pool. He had swum a few lengths. Then paced around the pool. And finally, he was simply sat in the shallow end looking out at the horizon. Sid wandered over to join him. He sat down in the water.

"Gosh it's cold," he grimaced.

"You get used to it after a while," said Tom, distantly. "You sort of acclimatise. Become institutionalised."

Sid realised that he wasn't talking about the water temperature.

"I mean, two years of working your arse off at school. Then six years at med school. Then God knows how many hours for the next few years. They move you. Every bloody six months. If it won't fit in one carload, it goes in the bin. You become so desensitised. They close the canteen at nights and weekends. They give you the shittiest accommodation and food. You have to suck up to the most unpleasant, personality disordered bastard bosses who then give you a crap reference with a smile when you leave. You finally get a steady job, or so you think. Then they split you up with so many bloody different Government reforms. And you lose the ability to have a meaningful relationship anymore. You have kids who hate you because you're always late home. And in a bad mood. And you can hardly blame your wife for buggering off either." He paused momentarily. "And then finally, they charge you for the honour of being struck off because you're depressed and addicted and a skeleton of who you were when you started out, young and naïve. No fucking wonder we're such a messed up profession. It's so... lonely."

He looked at Sid. Like a helpless, lost child. And then he did something he hadn't managed to do for a very long time. He sobbed. Sid wasn't quite sure how to react. And so he simply sat next to Tom for a few minutes. Then he finally reached across and put his hand on Tom's shoulder.

"It'll be ok," he said quietly. "There are still a lot of good people out there. And the patients aren't a bad bunch really."

Tom looked at his friend. "There's the irony, Sid. I really liked the patients. It shouldn't be like this. How do you cope?"

Sid smiled back. There was a brief pause. "Oh, I don't cope at all," he replied simply. "I just hope. But for once, I do feel a bit hopeful that better things lie ahead for all three of us."

*

Sid had finally coaxed Tom back to join the others on the sunbeds.

"You ok, Tom?" asked Dave.

"Not really mate, but thanks for asking. How about you?"

"Well, Tom, I can't say it's a great surprise. I've heard whispers on the hospital grapevine for a while that the Government were trying to privatise the service. But I have to say, the method beggars even my beliefs."

"So do you have a wise and clever plan?" Sid leaned over.

"My understanding of the accompanying documents in Lexy's file is that we doctors are to blame. We're greedy, incompetent, and uncaring, according to the minister. And therefore an easy target to allow the kind, caring, highly ethical private sector to rescue the situation."

"Knights in shining armour."

"Lots of knights, and a few new ones, including our RMC

chief." Tom twisted his face in disgust.

"Yes, but I can't imagine that the whole RMC are on his side. Surely the lay members have more sense." This comment came from Lexy, who had now put her book down.

"I think the whippet represents them," said Sid. "And I suspect that our man at the top has some hold over him about something. Some misdemeanours or personal secret of some sort."

"Well, he's clearly gay," said Lexy. The three looked at Lexy in surprise.

"Believe me, I'd know," she said. "He doesn't treat me like a piece of meat. And he likes my shoes. Gay men are usually much better company too."

"But this is 2018," said Dave. "Why would being gay be any kind of big deal to anyone anymore?"

"To most of us, it wouldn't be an issue at all. But maybe it is for him?" she replied.

"I think there may be something else," said Tom. "Apart from sex, what are the other biggest causes of scandals out there."

There was a pause.

"Money?" asked Dave. "Fraud?"

"Power and control?" added Sid. "In India, especially."

"Deceit," said Lexy. "Lies. Pretending to be something that you're not. Let's imagine the whippet has been employed to do a job. An important one for the RMC. And it turns out that he isn't as expert as he pretends. Then something goes badly wrong, and our man with the bowtie finds out. Add that to something else. Maybe some dodgy past. And bingo, you have a slave. Someone who has to dig around for you to get information and cover up for your own misdeeds."

The three men looked at Lexy in stunned silence. "Sorry. I read a lot of books" she said.

"I liked Scooby Doo too!" said Dave. They laughed.

"I think Lexy might be right," said Tom finally. "So he's blackmailing the whippet over something so that he can fulfil his own desires. In his case, a knighthood. Power and influence, to make up for his unsuccessful medical and legal career."

"And he, in turn, is the slave of the minister, who holds the key to his knighthood, provided that he tells the minister exactly what the minister wishes to hear."

"Maybe to forward his own career too?" added Sid.

"Yes," said Tom. "Let's imagine his party have some deeply vested interests in the private sector themselves. Political suicide to break up the NHS. Unless they simply have to because the doctors have broken it and it now needs fixing. Pick the one bunch of professionals that the public still has trust in and then systematically destroy it. Who's left? Oh gosh, it must be ProperDocs Ltd or some other unlikely creation, owned by some influential plc. Maybe even an American one."

Lexy looked alarmed now. "So, what about us poor patients? Those of us who can't diagnose ourselves and can't afford private insurance either?"

"Simply a gap in the market I expect. Collateral damage," said Tom, with bitterness. "It's going to be like the good old U.S. of A. A mixture of lots of homeless people coughing up new mutations of TB, and an elite of very rich people who can choose their own favourite antibiotics by text."

There was silence for a while.

"Surely the public won't buy it," said Dave, finally.

"Dave," Tom shot back with vehemence. "Tell me honestly that you didn't vote for this bloody Government. And you're supposed to have a higher IQ than most of the population! Lower tax rate?"

There was a pause.

"Tom, perhaps you need to be less angry with Dave," Sid

said, finally. "You have a very good point, but it's not his fault. We need to work together. Don't we, Lexy?" He turned to look at her. She nodded in agreement.

"We're a team."

"We're the Crash Team," added Dave with a grin. Tom smiled slightly. There was another pause. His face softened.

"Dave, you were always brilliant in the crash team in the hospital. You were the cavalry. I'm sorry, I'm just a bit messed up. Sorry mate. I shouldn't have said that."

"I was a prick, but I could save lives," replied Dave modestly. The tension in the atmosphere eased.

"Oi, you lot. Someone died?" It was Rhiannon with Ann. "Whatever it is, I bet it can't beat teaching fifteen little brats to play water polo without drowning each other. I need a swim. Tom? Sid?" She smiled at Dave. "Even you, Mr handsome-in-a-slightly-knackered-way?"

"Mr Handsome 1989, but now slightly-knackered, at your service ma'am," he replied gallantly. "And look, I even have new swim attire, befitting my near pensionable status." His swim shorts were now presentable. The budgie was caged. She laughed. He was still a charming old bugger, she thought to herself. She smiled at him. The budgie twitched, unseen.

Sid looked at Lexy. "Would you like to join us?" he asked.

"Not just yet," she replied. "My book's getting to the steamy bit." She laughed. "In a Jane Austen sort of way."

She had decided that Sid was the good-natured Mr Bingley in her book. Dave was definitely Wickham, but she couldn't fathom out whether Tom was Mr Darcy or simply from the local asylum.

CHAPTER TEN: PRIORITIES

"The living take priority over the dead."

Tom couldn't remember exactly why he had suddenly recalled this, but it had struck a chord. It had been a whole, albeit brief, seven-word long chapter in some junior doctors' survival guide he had read in panic shortly before starting his first job. At first, he hadn't understood its significance. No further explanation had been offered in the book, which had been a concise bible for the unwitting entering the unknown. He'd remembered the look of relief he'd received when the incumbent predecessor of his new medical houseman job had handed him the bleep.

"This is the crash bleep. You're on call today," he'd been told. "Good luck. You'll need it. The gerry ward is bloody miles away, by the way." Tom subsequently discovered that this meant the geriatric ward, subsequently relabelled *'Medical Elderly'*.

And that had been it. His handover. Crisp white coat around shoulders, stethoscope around neck. Survival bibles in pockets. A lucky gonk atop a pen in his upper pocket and a red hat pin through his lapel. The very picture of new cannon fodder for the medical department.

"God, you look young," said the sister in charge of the first ward - female general medicine. "Who's your boss?"

He'd answered.

She'd pulled a sympathetic face. "You'll be fine," she'd added, unconvincingly. "Ward round in thirty minutes. Take lots of notes and don't say too much." She gave him a second sympathetic look and walked back down the ward.

He was aware of a small group of pretty, young-looking nurses giggling in the corner and looking at him. He attempted a smile in return. More giggling followed. These were clearly the student nurses, and he appeared to be the object of their mirth. Finally, the boldest of the group came forward.

"Hello, Dr um," she read his name badge. "Lawrence. You the one from Arabia?" The other students giggled.

"Not unless it's near Wigan, darling," came the jaunty reply from behind him. "Now then, lovely ladies. please form an orderly queue. Dr Lawrence here will be at your cervix when he's finished his first on-call shift. Happily, I will be in the mess later!"

Tom turned around. A tall, rakish, good looking man in a white coat was stood just behind him. Somehow, this doctor had managed to make the white coat look like cool apparel. Tom was a mix of irritated yet impressed with his bravado.

"Death, taxes and a student nurse," he'd whispered into Tom's ear. Tom look puzzled. "The three certainties in life for a newly qualified doctor." He'd grinned in response. "You'll learn." And Tom had found his nervousness ease. The nurses had regrouped.

"Dave," he'd said simply and proffered his hand. "Medical SHO here for another month and then I officially become a gasman. I'm here to minimise the excess death rate expected this month and to resuscitate any of your cockups in the meantime," he added. Tom waited for the punchline. None arrived.

Dave continued amiably. "August 1st. Definitely not a day to become ill. Nor February 1st, for that matter. New doc's on the block… " He left the sentence hanging.

"The tall one's dirty as hell by the way, but you'll need some penicillin afterwards." He gestured towards the gaggle of nurses. The tall one scowled back. She looked very sexy, though, Tom had thought guiltily.

"And remember," Dave had said. "The living take priority over the dead. And don't shit on your own doorstep."

Tom had looked baffled.

"I'll translate. Don't go off signing a death certificate when somebody who's still alive and ill needs you, and don't shag anyone working on your team."

He tapped his nose. "Wise words you won't learn from *The Lancet*."

Fifteen further minutes or so passed. Finally, entourage almost complete, the bespectacled consultant had appeared.

"Shall we?" he asked the nursing sister in the dark blue, gallantly. And the ward round began. There was clearly a hierarchy of sorts to the procession that followed Dr Adams around the ward. Dr Adams appeared a genial sort. He started every new consultation with "Good morning, ma'am, what brings you here?"

"A big ambulance," said the first startled looking patient, as a ripple of mirth went around the group. The loudest from Tom's other houseman colleague. Dr Adams' look of patient condescension towards the lady was noted.

"No, I mean, why are you here, dear?" He said this at increased volume on the presumption that his initial vague question hadn't been heard properly by the lady.

"He's a nice fellow really," Dave had whispered to Tom.

That's good because he sounds like a condescending old twat, had thought Tom.

"I couldn't breathe properly," she'd said. "I think it's my heart doctor. That's why they brought me here."

"We're here to decide that," Dr Adams had replied, turning around self-importantly, and eliciting more appreciative murmurs of amusement from the group. Tom thought of his own mother, who disliked hospitals and couldn't hear very well. She'd tell you to go and fuck off, he thought to himself. His mouth lifted at the edges at the thought of this for a moment.

"So Dr, eh, Lawrence. What do we need to ask Mrs Arbuckle next?" Tom was now a rabbit in headlights. Dr Adams waited impatiently. "Oh, come, come, don't they teach you anything at medical school these days?" He rolled his eyes. "Anyone?"

"How long for? Ever had it before? What sets it off? What eases it? Any associated chest pains? How sudden in onset?"

Tom looked at his fellow houseman, reeling off a long and irritatingly correct textbook answer. Dr Adams was clearly impressed. "Well done, young… " he squinted at the badge, "Reynoldson. Good! a different medical school, I assume from young… " Adams gestured vaguely at Tom.

"Lawrence" replied Reynoldson helpfully, with a cheery grin. "And no, sir. Same one. He must have missed the lecture! Perhaps you were hungover, Tom?" He laughed, boomingly.

Tom hated his new work colleague already. It wasn't a good start. They'd be together working side by side for the next six months.

"Thank you," said Tom. Arse licker, he thought.

The round continued. Tom noticed that the 'to do' list was getting longer. Blood tests to take. Investigations to arrange. He hadn't even heard of some of them. He started to flag, and his mind wandered. The patients were of two types. Some were clearly very genuine, anxious about being in hospital, and looked at the entourage of faces for any sign of humanity and kindness. They found this mainly from the nursing staff. The others were what Dave called the 'airmilers'. These were the patients who seemed to have spent the majority of their adult lives in medical institutions of one sort or another. They seemed to thrive upon illness and its many varied presentations - a cat and mouse game of how to retain a hospital bed with inherent twenty-four hour care, before the doctors finally twigged that the origin of any illness lay somewhere above the roof of the mouth. Dr Adams was also slightly deaf, and Dave managed to take advantage of this when asked questions.

"How should we treat this young lady?" Dr Adams asked regarding the elderly Mrs Boston, a particularly successful airmiler, who had learnt the secret of charming the senior doctor with a combination of compliments and baffling headaches.

"Intracranial lead therapy?" suggested Dave quietly. Tom snorted.

"Sorry, didn't quite hear that Dr Ravensburg."

"Indian cranial-head therapy," he replied a little louder with a poker face. "It's supposed to very good for tension headaches and migraines."

He winked wickedly at Mrs Boston.

"Yes, yes, worth a try. Ask physio to see her. Sorry Mrs Boston, you can't go home yet."

Mrs Boston beamed. Fortunately, she hadn't heard the first suggestion either.

"Next... "

The crowd shuffled on. Heart failure. Overdose. Uncontrolled fits. Another overdose, this one a medically serious one. Chest infection. God knows what. Airmiler. Another airmiler. Chest pains. Finally, after almost two and a half hours, the round was over.

Tom sighed with relief. His houseman colleague was talking earnestly to the great man about some obscure paper he'd read about Indian head massage in the treatment of headaches in the *British Medical Journal.* Tom looked down miserably at his huge list of scribbled notes and required tasks.

"Not sure Mrs Boston would quite have understood the bullet through the head suggestion, but that wasn't as bad as I thought." It was the tall student nurse from earlier. "Hey, when you've finished your mountain of tasks, we're having a party this Friday night in the nurses' digs. You can bring your friend too. And a bottle of something."

She walked away but turned around again. "I don't mean the clever shit one. I mean the comedian. Tell him he owes me a blow job." She gave him a little wink and walked away.

Bloody hell, thought Tom. Your lives in our hands…

And then an insistent set of shrill pips had sounded from the bleep clipped to his pocket. CARDIAC ARREST WARD 5. CARDIAC ARREST WARD 5. Another set of shrill pips. A stark reminder that this was a serious job. And then a sudden race. An exhilarating, terrifying dash down the ward and along the corridors. A flash of white coats with stethoscopes flapping around necks. Tom and Dave had arrived first. Followed by the anaesthetist and then the porter, pushing the 'crash trolley', containing the essential means of maintaining life.

"Sorry, sorry, his leads came off. Student nurse called the crash team by mistake."

"False alarm. Thanks, everyone. Sorry."

The embarrassed looking senior nurse from the ward turned around in search of the unfortunate student. A timid new girl from Manchester.

"Oops," said Dave. Tom looked relieved. "Lunch?" continued Dave. "Man cannot live on love alone."

Chapter Eleven: Book Lovers

In Tenerife, the sun was still shining. Tom now hadn't had an alcoholic drink in almost two weeks, and he felt so much healthier. He had anticipated cravings but hadn't really had any. Apart from when he had learnt the news of the RMC files. Dave was asleep. Dreaming of Rhiannon. In his dreams, she couldn't resist his charms. Sid, who was prone to fretting. Was fretting. He was aware that he had left his wife and home in a hurry. His wife would be furious. Partly, because he wasn't dead, which would have automatically triggered his life insurance policies, allowing her to publicly weep for her lost husband, and then move in with her lover of the past ten years. But also because she had now lost her main source of income and the easiest target for both her anger and better throwing arm. Sid worried that this anger might have been transferred to his son, who resembled his father in physical appearance.

He texted his son again. I am safe and ok. How are you? I miss you. All will be well. Please reply. This was probably the twentieth text he had sent. No replies so far. But then a reply came. *WHERE ARE YOU, YOU PATHETIC BASTARD OF A HUSBAND? YOU HAVE RUINED ALL OF OUR LIVES.*

Sid grimaced. His wife had clearly confiscated his son's phone. He had no option but to block the number. He had already blocked his wife's. An hour or so passed and a new message appeared. This one simply asked, *WHERE R U DAD.* He didn't recognise the number. He hesitated. He sent a question mark in reply.

DAD, IT'S ANIL. MUM'S GOT MY PHONE. SHE'S TOLD THE POLICE YOU'VE GONE MISSING. WE'RE OK. MUM SAME AS. WHAT DID YOU DO?! DON'T ANSWER BY TEXT! USUAL EMAIL SAFE. MUM CAN'T HACK IT. KEEP IN TOUCH.

PS ENJOY TENERIFE :) (PHONE TRACKER ON, YOU NEED TO INACTIVATE IT. MUM HASN'T TWIGGED YET)

MISS YOU

A XX

Sid looked a mixture of relief and alarm. He looked in panic at his phone. He turned to Lexy, who was still reading her book.

"Lexy, do you know anything about phones? I need to inactivate a thing called a tracker."

Lexy looked up. "I didn't realise Mr Bingley had a smartphone," she said with a smile. He smiled back.

"I'd be very grateful if Miss Bennett would save me from debtor's prison or the workhouse."

She smiled again. He had such a lovely, intelligent, and kind face.

"I'm not Elizabeth'" she said.

"I'd hoped not," he replied. "I prefer Jane."

"Darcy needs an Elizabeth, though. He's rather lost at the moment."

They looked across at Tom. Tom was on his phone. He

was intermittently writing and then searching for something. Presumably on the internet. Oblivious to the pretty girls who sunbathed around him, within an easy surreptitious glance.

"My son has texted me. I think. My wife has his phone."

Lexy frowned. "So, you're married then?" (She already knew this, of course.)

"On paper still," replied Sid. "A long story. My wife hates me. Thinks I'm pathetic. Arranged marriage before I left India to work in Scotland. Neither one of us each other's choice. No better for her really."

"Scotland?" she said. "What was that like? Did you suffer from racism there?" she asked.

"No, not really. They're not racist there unless you're from England. Then it's acceptable!" They both smiled.

"How many children do you have?" she asked.

"Just the one. Anil, eighteen and about to go to university to study business studies in London. He texted me to say that my phone can be tracked!"

"Is he like you, Anil?" She leant over. "Put your password in first," she instructed. Sid smelt a soft fragrance of Chanel mixed with sun cream. He closed his eyes for a second and breathed in through his nose. She smelt lovely.

"Right, I've deactivated it," she said. "You're safe now!"

"So, are you planning to divorce at some stage?" He detected a slightly more urgent note in her voice.

"She threatens to, but then she never mentions it again for a while. It's so complicated in Indian culture. Most of the couples I know just pretend all is well in public and then scream at each other in private and have a lover hidden somewhere else."

"Are you 'most couples'? Do you have some lover tucked away?"

He smiled at her. "No. She does. She calls him her

handyman actually. But no. I think I'm a little older fashioned. I'm not looking for a quick. Um…"

"Consummation? Shag?" she added helpfully, smiling at his embarrassment.

"Well, yes, you could call it that."

"So if I offered you one now, you'd turn me down."

Sid's mouth fell open. He mouthed something.

"Oh, Sid, I'm teasing you!" She laughed. "Come on. Darcy's just dived into the lake in my book. Let's do the same here." She stood up, took her hat off and dived gracefully into the pool by their side.

"Oh my god, that's bloody cold," she spluttered, as she surfaced with a laugh. Sid jumped in too. He was feeling hot and bothered. Lexy splashed him. "I can't quite figure you out. There must be a lot of anger hidden in you somewhere, but you never seem to show it. It's eating Tom up. Oozing out of every pore. Dave's brain has some sort of short circuit I think to protect him but... But you. You're a thinker. And a gentleman. And a—"

To her huge surprise, Sid suddenly walked towards her in the pool, put his arms around her waist, and kissed her fully on the mouth with a rawness and passion. It was clumsy and amateur, but Lexy felt like she had been kissed with real meaning for the first time in her life. She gasped. They broke apart briefly.

"Oh my god!" said Sid "I don't know what came over me, I'm so sorry, I—"

She kissed him back this time. She caressed his head and tousled his hair as their mouths met. Then opened. And for almost a minute, they simply remained locked together in a deep, loving embrace. Sid felt like he was melting. Tears streamed from his eyes, hidden by the water running down his face.

Lexy put one finger to her lips and shook her head slightly. "Shush," she said gently. "Don't break the spell."

She beckoned him to follow her, and she climbed gracefully out of the pool. Sid followed her. No one else had been watching them. They went into the hotel. Hand in hand like teenage lovers. And the ripples in the pool area ebbed away discreetly, leaving the surface perfectly flat once again.

*

Meanwhile in an oak filled office in London, the bowtied man from the RMC was looking worried.

"Where the bloody hell did you leave them?" he demanded of his anxious, wiry 'junior', Myles, sat across from him. "You do realise this is all your fault."

The junior sat stiffly in the opposite chair. He knew it was pointless to argue with his boss.

"Those files could be any bloody where by now. In the wrong hands…" He left his sentence hanging.

"Are you quite sure that you, I mean we, had them in the pub the last time you saw them?" Myles ventured apprehensively.

"Bloody sure of it. There was only you. And me. A few regulars who look like they'll meet their maker soon."

"And the bar manager, Lexy."

"Ah yes, Lexy. Pretty girl. In a sort of Suzi Quatro come Cher sort of way."

"Nice shoes," added his colleague.

"You poofters are all the same," retorted his boss, sharply and unnecessarily.

Myles started internally but said nothing for a while. "I understand she left shortly afterwards, jetting off somewhere fairly exotic."

"Where?" asked his boss. "And how the hell do you know?"

"One of the Spanish islands, I think. She said something to the postman after he brought her a postcard. *Hasta la vista baby*. It's from a film."

"Good god, man, no one sends postcards anymore these days," he scoffed. "They text. Or email. Or Skype or whatever these bloody phones can do nowadays."

"Unless you don't know the person's email or phone number," added the wiry man.

"Myles, that is a thought," said his boss. "Maybe she's buggered off with one of the regulars."

Myles was astonished. His boss almost never called him by his first name.

"I doubt it. She's always getting chatted up, and she just ignores them. Or tells them to bugger off in no uncertain terms." He paused. "But maybe one of the less regulars might be more her type," added Myles. "Maybe even one of our boys?"

The RMC boss paled visibly. "Oh, bloody hell!" he said. "You don't suppose it's one of the ones from the list? Or even all three...?"

They looked at each other. Recognition dawning.

"Right, come with me." He stood up quickly. "Time for a pint, I think. Let's see if she left any clues behind the bar. It might be time for a little trip to the sun for you Myles."

He looked at his minion's dubious expression.

"On expenses of course."

*

Rhiannon , Ann, Tom, and Dave were sat in the bar area when Sid and Lexy walked back in together. The light was fading. Dave gave Rhiannon a puzzled look, and she silenced him with a simultaneous and threatening lowering of both eyebrows.

"Hey you two! Fancy some food?" she asked.

"Yes," they both answered in unison. Tom noticed they were looking guilty, like a pair of naughty schoolchildren.

"Looks like you both might need some sustenance," added Tom with a smile. This time they giggled, nervously. A moment passed.

"Well, I think it's lovely," said Ann. "Romance isn't dead."

"Right, you teenagers, food time," announced Rhiannon. She couldn't quite hide an edge of irritation in her voice. "I'm starving." She looked at Dave. "And you can buy me a cocktail."

"Yes, boss!" he replied. "Yikes. What's got into her?" He mumbled to Tom.

"I think it's perhaps what hasn't got into her," replied Tom very quietly. "Have you ever considered wooing a girl the old-fashioned way?"

Dave look startled.

"Bloody hell, Dave. Did you just skip that chapter?"

Now Dave looked hurt.

"Dave, I think you just need to imagine that your brain, for once, has some control over your groin area and that perhaps even modern girls appreciate a little romance and courting, rather than feeling like some sort of prize heffa in a show."

"I really like Rhiannon," whispered Dave defensively. The others were now chattering away, oblivious to the pep talk occurring in their midst.

"I know. But she just thinks you want to shag her."

"Well, I do. But not like that. It's different. Oh shit."

"Are you suggesting that for the first time in your life, you might actually want something more meaningful than your usual overnight relationship?"

"I was married once you know," replied Dave. Tom looked at him. And said nothing.

Tom turned around to interrupt the others. "I think cocktails are an excellent idea," he said. "But Rhiannon, Dave here has just told me that he would like to take you for a cocktail. Just the two of you and the rest of us will join you later. He's going to put on that new shirt you chose for him and have a shower and a shave first. Aren't you, Dave? And he'll meet you in thirty minutes at the main door, as he thinks you look just lovely as you are."

He turned to Dave.

"Um yes, just that's about it," said Dave.

Rhiannon beamed back. "That sounds lovely!"

"And we'll join you for food around half eight if that's ok?" said Tom. "Ann, could you invite Diego too? It'd be a shame to leave him out. He's part of the family."

Ann beamed. "I think he may be working, but I'll ask him to join us later if he is."

"Right. Dave. Twenty-nine minutes left. Off you go."

Dave got up obediently. He actually looked nervous. "Tom, have you got any decent aftershave I can borrow?"

Tom smiled. "Of course. It's on the shelf in the bathroom. I think your need is greater than mine. Just don't go and drown yourself in it. Three squirts says subtle. Six exudes desperation. Remember, women generally have a more refined olfactory system than men."

Dave left the pool. The three walked back into the lobby together, leaving Sid and Tom together. Tom broke the silence.

"She's a lovely girl, Sid."

"She is so beautiful," replied Sid wistfully. "In every way. It's been such a long time. Since I… Since I've…"

"Been in love," finished Tom for him.

"Yes. I feel like my insides are on fire."

"Sure it's not something you ate?" They both laughed.

"How about you, Tom?" Sid asked.

"I think I'm a bit too bitter and twisted still," replied Tom. "It's a bit like believing in Father Christmas for me. It's a bit of a bugger when you realise it's just make-believe. Particularly when you believed in it. Utterly."

"But Christmas isn't really about Father Christmas, is it?" replied Sid. "I thought the Christmas message was something else altogether. Perhaps you just believed in the wrong bit of it."

Tom turned to look at his friend. "Sid, why are you always so bloody wise?" He clearly meant it. "You don't seem bitter about anything. You just accept things."

"I'm Hindu," said Sid. "It's the basis of the religion. Karma. You try to do good and eventually good things will follow."

"I thought that was Buddhism," replied Tom.

"Karma is the thread of most religions, Tom. I'm not even very religious. But I do believe in Karma. You're sad and angry. And your anger spills out. It spoils your life for you."

"I'm sorry," said Tom.

"No need," said Sid. "Just try to lose the anger. Retarget it into something positive."

"You look ten years younger, Sid. Weren't you worried that…?"

Sid laughed. "I should have been bloody terrified! But it didn't seem to matter at all. It was like we'd known each other for years. It's so strange. I wasn't even nervous in the end. It wasn't about the performance. It was about the intimacy. And it was… " He looked into the distance. "It just felt right."

"What are you going to do about your own marriage?" asked Tom. "Isn't it complicated?"

"Do you know, Tom, for the first time in my life, I'm not worried. My wife doesn't love me. Never did. I'll make sure she is ok. But it's time for me to move on now. And start to live my life. At my age, fifty-four. It's ridiculous, isn't it? And she needs to live hers too. She's not a bad woman. She's just dissatisfied. And angry."

"We'd be a great match!" laughed Tom. "By the way, that was definitely a joke!"

"You're probably much more her type," smiled Sid. "You wouldn't put up with any of her shit!"

Tom looked surprised. "Sid, I've never heard you swear before!" he exclaimed. "That's twice in two minutes!"

"Maybe we're not so different after all," he said. "Come on. Let's get a hot chocolate with the others."

And the two walked together back to the main lobby. Sid put his arm around his friend's shoulder. Tom wasn't used to physical contact. But this felt brotherly and strangely comforting. He put his own arm around his friend.

"Do you know? If I were the slightest bit queer, I'd marry you Sid!"

"And if I was the slightest bit queer that'd make me the luckiest man alive!" replied Sid.

"Does your Lexy have a friend for me?" They both laughed again.

*

Half eight arrived, and they all met for food. Diego was working, but he'd suggested a small restaurant on the outskirts of the resort, and said he'd join them later. The restaurant was very difficult to find. It looked closed from the outside, and they walked past it twice before a head popped out of the door to beckon them in. The proprietor was Spanish and clearly spoke no English at all, but they managed to order a carafe of red wine, bread, and a large bowl of olives.

"I think it's tapas here," said Rhiannon. "Pick and mystery mix. Are you guys game for it?"

"I'm vegetarian," replied Sid. "But I'm happy to share anything without meat in it."

And so the courses arrived. Accompanied by smiles and sign language mainly. Dave sat next to Rhiannon, and she scolded him gently at times for his table manners, but there was clearly a new warmth between them too. She undid his top button.

"It suits you, she said. I like you in blue."

Ann shot Tom a sideways glance. "It must be something in the water," she said.

Some dishes were meat or fish-based. Others clearly vegetarian. Six or seven dishes later, a dessert arrived. Delicious vanilla flan with a sweet caramel sauce and almond Turron, a sweet candy-like biscuit served with hot black coffee and a small orange liqueur.

They looked at each other. "Wow! I'd never have spotted this place in a million years!" said Dave. He looked at Rhiannon. "It's fit for a princess."

"Cheesy, but it's a start," she said. "You're not quite Shakespeare yet, but I guess I'm no Desdemona either."

"I think you are," said Dave. He clearly had no idea who Desdemona was, but he hid it well. Tom shrugged at Ann but still smiled.

"Othello," whispered Sid helpfully. "Perhaps don't stab her to death, though."

"I don't know much opera," replied Dave, absently.

A noise from behind them signalled the arrival of Diego. Ann beamed and stood up to kiss him. The host, and his wife both hugged him and produced another carafe of wine, along with soft drinks for Tom and Sid. They all sat at the table together. Finally, Tom broke the reverie.

"Right, crash team members. We have been here on this amazing island for nearly two weeks, but we haven't really explored it yet. And we still don't have a clear plan as to how long we can stay here before we either run out of cash or get arrested or both."

"May I suggest firstly, a toast?" They raised their glasses to their hosts. "*Salud*!"

"Secondly, apologies for being such a miserable old git. I plan to enter a chrysalis phase very soon and emerge as a butterfly, or at least a decent looking moth. Thank you for your patience and friendship!"

"To butterflies and moths!" they all toasted. They tried to ignore the electric zing as a moth was simultaneously electrocuted by the insect killer in the corner.

"Hopefully, that one was wearing rubber soles."

"To our soles," replied Dave, raising his glass with a grin.

"Thank you to our new poet laureate," replied Tom. "And finally, here's to our futures. Whatever they may be. May we accept them and embrace them. With wit, bonhomie, and courage!"

An enthusiastic mumble followed.

"Ok, to the future!"

"The future!" they all cheered back in unison. Ann kissed Diego. Rhiannon kissed Dave. Lexy and Sid kissed each other. Tom looked a lonely figure for a moment. His thoughts drifted momentarily, and he had a brief glimpse of the girl wearing his cool-and-crazy t-shirt. He had no idea why. And then the host and his wife hugged him too.

"*El Futuro*!" announced Tom with a grin. This time, with gusto!

CHAPTER TWELVE: DR DAVID RAVENSBURG'S STORY

David had been a late developer. At school, he was shy, spotty, and invisible. The private boys' school, to which his parents had sent him at the age of eleven, had a well-known reputation for educational excellence, and a less well-known reputation for bullying and abuse. He'd spent five generally miserable years there, successfully dodging the perverts but not always the bullies. To survive, you needed to develop a larger-than-life personality or become a bully or pervert yourself. David had become Dave the Rave. Class comedian. Artful dodger. Legend of larking about. Liked by all but properly known by very few. He'd learnt that natural charm, a witty retort, and a cheeky grin could extricate him from most circumstances. Make 'em laugh and they won't hit you or try to bugger you. Staff or pupils.

His parents were blissfully unaware of all of this, of course. His mother was a headteacher, whilst his father was a skilled barrister. Arguing your point in his household was simply a waste of time. His mother always won. He had no siblings, and although he didn't recognise it, his childhood had been a lonely one. They hadn't gone hungry. The rows were mainly conducted behind closed doors and involved his father's indiscretions, both at the legal Bar and behind the local bar. A smiling face was presented to Dave by his mother. She was rarely affectionate with him, but that was more frequent than his father, who was critical and stern by nature and in practice.

At the age of seventeen, Dave had been sat in the school library - usually a safe haven for the victimised in the school, under the watchful eye of a Welsh dragon called Mrs Evans. Dave never usually entered the library, but his A-levels were looming, and he was seeking an escape from his hometown. He had wanted to become a vet originally, but his chemistry teacher had told him in no uncertain terms to set his sights lower based on his expected grades. And so he had opted for medicine instead.

"You've a chance of three Bs if you get the right questions, Ravensburg. Though god help humanity if you succeed."

"If I don't get in, I could always try teaching," he'd replied with a grin. The resulting detention had been worth it. And so he'd scoured the student feedback forms from the various 'Old Lankys' who had dug their escape tunnels successfully and got 'over or under the wire' to universities around the country. Some questionnaires had already been pre-vetted for any signs of dissent or criticism of the school, but most described the sheer joy of escape to educational freedom.

A few had caught his eye, particularly the one from Richard Short. The boy with the worst Acne in the school at the time. It's ace here. Lectures aren't compulsory, more skirt than trousers at the uni and even I have a girlfriend now. Vidi ,Vici, Veni!

Dave knew enough Latin to get his joke. Perhaps she'd even been called Vicky.

Girls eh? The thing of dreams to an existing Lanky. Lanky being the nickname of pupils from their school in Lancashire. The local comprehensive school children had amusingly changed the L to a W, although credit really belonged to Dave himself, who had spontaneously coined the phrase to soothe the wrath of a gang that had cornered him on the way home from school one day. They'd ended up sharing cigarettes and slapping him on the back.

Yes, he'd decided that his future lay in the university that satisfied the criteria of being both as far away from his father as possible and offering the statistically highest likelihood of him getting laid. A summer holiday the year before in France had offered a glimpse of the future. Two weeks of sunshine had completely cleared his acne, and the beaches had been littered with gorgeous French women, mostly lying topless on the sand, or frolicking in the surf, seemingly oblivious to their astonishing natural beauty and grace.

One of the girls on the campsite had taken a fancy to him, and they had spent many evenings fumbling and kissing in the sand dunes at dusk. It had been an awakening for him. Dave felt that his future lay in being a doctor. Or at least in being frequently laid as a doctor. And so his grades had soared. He was now due straight 'As' in all three sciences.

"Have you considered taking the Oxbridge exams?" his biology teacher had asked.

"Their medical courses don't really have the content that I'm looking for," he'd replied honestly. Cambridge, in particular, seemed to offer the lowest statistical prospect of a shag. At least of the heterosexual type that he was seeking. And so Dave had finished his final year, gained four inches in height, and graduated with the predicted 'A' grades. He thanked each teacher in person and grinned broadly at his chemistry teacher, who had simply said, "You lucky, lucky bastard Ravensburg". Dave assumed he had meant the grades, although his teacher had actually meant for the successful escape attempt.

Medical school had been harder than he'd expected. He'd partied a little too hard in the first year at Edinburgh and had needed resits to remain in the course. The students had also been more serious than he had expected, but by year three, they had reached the clinical years, and now the sweetie shop was well and truly open. Dave the Rave had soaked himself in pretty girls. Most had participated willingly, fully in the knowledge of his transparent goals. Whilst others had hoped that he might change, and that they would become the chosen one, and 'bag a doctor'.

Unfortunately, the sheer quantity and brevity of his flings had made it difficult for him to differentiate any real feelings from the sheer thrill of the chase. Women initially found him fascinating but later discovered that his affections were limited to the few brief minutes before and immediately after copulation.

"Have you ever been in love?" his closest friend would ask.

"Almost every week for the last two years!" He'd reply.

Eventually, he'd made a girl pregnant, and her father had insisted that they married before the child was born. The nurse involved, Megan, had actually fallen for him in a major way, seemingly blind to his shallow traits and Lothario ways. She'd stuck by him for ten years. They'd even had two more children together, but his rakish good looks, the inherent sexual perils of the job and the large amount of free-flowing alcohol at medical parties had finally nailed the lid down on the coffin of his marriage. Contact with the children had initially been fairly frequent, but his reliability at picking them up on time, showing any real interest in their lives and finally, a very public naming in a local hospital scandal had sealed the fate on his relationship with them. He genuinely missed them. Sadly, they didn't miss him at all.

*

Dave sat by the pool, looking into the water. "You ok?" It was Tom. "Thought you'd be up to your balls in Rhiannon by now!"

Dave winced. "Please don't talk about her like that. And no, we just talked and walked along the beach after we left the restaurant. She's not like that."

"You bloody are," said Tom, with a scoff. "Unless you've had a frontal lobotomy overnight. Or been beamed up in a spaceship, with a replica in your place." He looked poignantly up at the sky. "Dave. Can you hear me up there?"

Dave carried on staring into the water. "Do you think I'm a transparent, heartless unfaithful bastard?"

Tom sat down by his side. "Honest answer?"

Dave pulled a face and sighed. "Yes, please, honest answer."

Tom paused. "I think you're transparent when it comes to women. Unfaithful, definitely, but heartless bastard? No. You're a bastard with a heart!"

Dave said nothing.

"Oh, for fuck's sake, Dave, don't lose your sense of humour on me! No, I don't think you're heartless or a bastard. I think you're addicted to sex and excitement and can't stop yourself from bagging another conquest. Anyway, why ask me? I'm hardly a shining example of anything?"

"Because you're basically an ordinary, decent guy."

"Thanks for the overwhelming endorsement," added Tom, drily. "You've pulled. Where shall I put my clothes?"

"No I mean it," said Dave. "You have a moral compass.

You follow it, even when it's inconvenient or uncomfortable. I fucked up big time. Megs was a decent girl. She wasn't bad in the sack either..."

Now Tom winced. "And my kids are grown up now and won't have anything to do with me."

"So how many women have you actually slept with? Or should I say, stayed up all night in bed with?"

Dave paused. Then groaned. "Oh god, well over a hundred."

Tom looked genuinely stunned. "No way!"

Dave now looked embarrassed. "I really can't remember, but an awful lot."

"Any particularly memorable?"

"Well, that's the problem. Sexually, yes, but not in any other way. None that left me feeling fulfilled. Just temporarily satiated, I guess."

"So why the crisis of conscience now?" asked Tom.

"Because I'm getting old. And fretful. I don't want to leave this planet having only shagged my way across the health services of Scotland and England with nothing other than stained bedsheets."

"Perhaps you could get a job in Wales?" suggested Tom. "And you've probably doubled sales of Daz too!"

"Tom, I'm being serious. Ok, so perhaps Rhiannon and I did a little more than just walk along the beach last night."

"So you don't need to work in Wales anymore?" asked Tom. He grinned mischievously.

"Well, it's clearly a waste of time pouring my soul out to you!" Dave got up to leave.

"Sorry, sit down, sit down," said Tom. "Come on." He patted the floor. "I apologise. Sorry. I'm just never quite sure when you're joking or not. So, what went wrong?"

"For the first time in my life, I couldn't do it."

"What do you mean? You mean you couldn't physically get an erection? They do tablets for that…"

"No, I mean it didn't feel the right time. I felt like I wanted to… get to know her better first?"

"She didn't swear and use the 'L' word, did she?"

"Love. Me? Oh, I doubt that. Why do you think she does?" he asked anxiously. He looked like a child, seeking approval.

Tom looked back up at the sky. "Bring Dave back, you bastards. He'll infect you all!" He turned back. "Dave, I haven't the foggiest idea. Would it scare the shit out of you if she said she did?"

Dave paused. "I think it probably would."

"Why this time, though? Isn't that part of the fix for you? They say they love you. Vici, I conquered. Just after Vidi and shortly before Veni?"

Dave looked sheepish. "Do you think I'm that shallow?"

"Of course!" replied Tom. "It's hard not to. Remember my girl? The student nurse who nicked my t-shirt at the party?"

Dave looked glum. "I'm sorry."

"Yeah, I bloody was too. Unlike you, I didn't shag the entire nursing school. She was nice. I really liked her."

There was silence for a few minutes.

"Rhiannon asked me if I wanted to make love to her. I haven't called it that for years. Fancy a shag is much less emotional."

"And did you. Did you want to?"

"Yes. Yes, I did, Tom. But not in a sleazy way. Properly. With romance and meaning. Like Sid. So I made some excuse about being tired. And I think she took major offence."

"Well, it's certainly a first for you. I can see why she was offended. Didn't you once even shag the cleaner when she accidentally woke you up in that on-call room?"

Dave's look of utter dejection even made Tom relent a

little.

"It's even worse with Sid and Lexy connecting as they do."

"So you spotted our two lovebirds sneak off from the pool yesterday too?"

"Oh shit, no. Did they really?"

"I think poor Sid must have emptied his entire soul into her yesterday. He's absolutely smitten with her."

"I think she might be too," said Dave sadly. "So what's his big secret?"

"He's the genuine article, Dave. He's decent, clever, kind, and honest. Much underestimated by all. And Lexy can simply see through his bumbling exterior."

"And Rhiannon?" asked Dave.

Tom paused. "She's a lovely girl. She's young. Can't be more than mid-twenties."

"She's twenty-seven," said Dave, defensively.

"I suspect she wants children. A husband. Someone to love her, even when her breasts start to sag and her tummy spills over her trousers. And her parents are infirm and need taking places. Not just some summer infatuation. Be honest. Ask yourself what you're really looking for."

"I don't know," said Dave simply. "Tom, I don't fucking know!"

"Then don't break her heart until you do, is my best advice," said Tom. "Or yours. I'd suggest a beer, but in my case, I simply don't think that would be a very good idea yet. So how about a freshly squeezed orange juice from the bar for the two of us. Please?"

Dave looked at his companion. Tom had lost some of his excess weight. His jowls were less swollen. He had a light tan, especially on his balding head. He looked relaxed and almost handsome.

"Orange juice it is. Single or double?"

CHAPTER THIRTEEN: RETURN TO BLIGHTY

At some point, the inevitable discussion needed to be held. The Crash Team, as they now fondly referred to themselves, had been formed only a fortnight earlier, and although their combined blood pressures, stress levels, and in Tom's case, liver function enzymes, had reduced considerably, practical problems on the home front couldn't be deferred indefinitely. For Sid, there was little left to do. His work contract had been automatically terminated by his employer on some small print, and his bank accounts had already been frozen by his wife, who had filed for divorce. Anil had messaged him about this by email the night before.

He had replaced his mobile phone, for one with a lesser ability to communicate via facial recognition or psychokinesis but a greater ability to make a phone call whilst retaining some remnant of charge. With the help of Lexy, he had managed to transfer his important contacts across to the new phone, along with the various passwords of important accounts and documents. He had then deleted any important data from the original, switched back on the location device and left it in the hands of one of Ann's friends, an air hostess, who had promised to leave it temporarily in various amusing locations overseas, whilst on charge. He also wanted to pick up his coin collection. He seemed quite insistent about that.

Tom was sanguine. He needed to clear his rented accommodation out, settle a few outstanding bills and set up some automatic direct debits. He had decided to keep his car and get it taxed and MOT'd for twelve months as a back-up. His friend had a farm and had agreed to store it for a minimal sum in one of the spare barns, where it would be visually hidden but road legal. He also needed some dental work, as a result of his previously poor diet and drinking habits, and to send some belated family birthday cards. He assumed that the health authority would have already moved his patients to the nearby new health facility, run by a local consortium of businessmen and fronted by a retired nurse with an OBE.

Dave announced that he didn't have any reason to go back. He had been living with a friend in England and could still access his considerable financial resources via the internet. Suspension meant full pay from his employer, although he was technically supposed to remain in the UK.

"They always take for bloody ever to investigate everything." He knew this from previous experience. He secretly also hoped that Rhiannon would start speaking to him again. She had been mysteriously 'busy' for the three days since their date had ended in a premature termination. Sadly, he concluded that he had nothing else to go back for. Ann and Rhiannon had no reason to return to Wales yet either. Lexy was undecided initially but decided to go with them. She had no family left in the UK, few belongings, and no motorbike, since the local gang near her home had stolen it for spare parts. Soon, the handlebars would decorate the wall of a new biker bar in Brixton.

The only thing she really wanted to do was to say goodbye to a couple of the locals who had been kind to her, and one of her two only real friends, a part-time cleaner at the pub. She was also aware that she would soon run out of money, and despite Sid's generosity and assurances, she wanted to retain her independence. She did have a small amount of savings hidden in a box at the back of her wardrobe. She'd also started to write a book in London and wanted to pick her notes up before they were thrown away, along with the rest of her few remaining belongings. And so, cheap flights had been booked. Returns, with a promise to meet up in seven days in the airport departure lounge. They hadn't bothered to take cases out. Hand luggage was ample. A supermarket carrier bag in Sid's case.

Meanwhile, another series of flights were being booked. Myles, who was terrified of flying, was booked on a flight to Tenerife South, ostensibly to attend a conference on 'Steering Groups and Savings to the Health Service Managerial Budget'. His boss had assured him that he wouldn't be away for long, though Myles noticed that the ticket was currently only one way. Another was being planned by Sid's wife. She had identified his phone's location and had bought her Turkish currency ready for the trip to Istanbul. She beamed to herself. Her lawyer would love this.

Diego and Dave had waved them goodbye at the airport. Ann and Rhiannon had been working. And so the Crash Team was separated for the first time in its short history. Dave was driven back to the hotel in Diego's clattering old Renault 5 and dropped at the main entrance with a cheery wave. A few discs in his spine had relocated slightly on the journey, courtesy of old

French suspension and some potholes. He went to the pool and sat down on a nearby chair. He looked at his feet. He looked at his abdomen. He felt the thinning crown on his head and he suddenly felt very old and very alone. A few minutes passed.

"Ey, *Señor*, where your friends?" Dave turned around. It was Eloy, the other barman. Devilishly handsome, immaculately coiffured and, Dave noted with irritation, with an entourage of adoring beauties sat at his bar.

"Come over, my friend. Is happy hour soon!"

"Great, I'll have two bottles of Prozac please," murmured Dave to himself, and slowly made his way over to Eloy's hareem. Three pints of lager later, Dave felt somewhat better. A girl from Liverpool had asked him if he had retired to Spain, and another had said he'd be perfect for her mum. He had smiled externally and groaned inwardly.

"Ey, *Señor*. You Rhiannon's friend, yes?"

"Yes, *sí*. I was," he replied.

"She very sad," said Eloy. "She work near here though. Hotel El Ole 2. Maybe you see her?"

"Ah, too late I think," said Dave sadly.

"I think maybe happy hour there soon for you!" he replied. "Go see her." Eloy winked at him. "She beautiful girl."

Dave was feeling both hot and a little drunk now. So he decided that perhaps a dip in an adjacent hotel pool might not be such a bad idea. And with any luck, she'd be in the pool with the kids. He could observe her from a safe distance. Maybe even saunter over and say hello.

*

A waiter came over to him and smiled. "Big beer, my friend?"

"Why not. Yes please," he replied. The sunbeds all had towels on them, so he chose a chair slightly in the shade, with a

115

view of the main pool but with an umbrella in the way. He could see her at the far end of the main pool, looking harassed in her bright orange t-shirt and yellow shorts. She was trying to organise two groups of children into water-polo-come-volleyball teams. It was like trying to herd cats. Feral ones at that.

He pulled the visor of his hat down slightly to avoid being seen. He furtively glanced across again. One of the feral pack, a small boy with the face of a partially edentulous rodent, had decided to slip away from the main group. He splashed some ice-cold pool water over an unwitting, snoring sunbather, and hid behind a palm tree, grinning, as the blonde victim sat bolt upright, uttering a loud "Fuck!". Not Norwegian then, and little bugger, thought Dave. It was quite funny, though.

Volleyballs were now regularly splashing more of the pool recliners, who were clearly becoming increasingly annoyed and moving away from the pool's edge. Towels draped over one arm and sun cream bottles sticking out dangerously from the other, they retreated like a beaten army. The rodent lost his prey.

"Bloody kids," muttered one elderly gentleman as he shuffled past.

Dave smiled back. "Yep, Brexit, planet destruction, traffic congestion… Bloody kids eh?"

Ratboy had finished rummaging through the ashtray near the exit gate and was now poking a wet stick into one of the broken light fittings near the pool. Dave watched with semi-drunken interest. He wondered where the child's parents were. He glimpsed through a gap in the parasols at Rhiannon. Harassed but still beautiful. She was trying to cajole, encourage and amuse her wild pack whilst also ensuring that none of them was drowning. He could see her counting them. And then her look of panic, as she realised that one was missing. He thought better of waving to her.

Meanwhile, Ratboy had now discovered exactly why the light was not working. With a small flash, he completed the circuit, shot gracefully into the air and with a beautiful arc of sparks, fell headfirst into the deep end of the pool. There was a shriek from a nearby guest as the ripples started to settle on the surface. Dave's brain immediately clicked. He launched himself from his chair, his newspaper landing neatly on the buttocks of a large nearby guest, and jumped into the pool, immediately regretting that he hadn't removed his shoes first.

He looked down into the depths and could just about see the outline of a small body towards the bottom of the pool. Dave was not a good swimmer, and the weight of his wet shirt and shoes surprised him, but he dived under the surface and grabbed about, trying to reach the child. Contact lenses are not particularly useful underwater either, and Dave struggled to see anything at all. He surfaced, gasping and spluttering. "Goggles!" He shouted. "Get me goggles!"

A pair were thrown at him. With great difficulty, and several mouthfuls of pool water later, he managed to get them on. They were luminous yellow and extremely tight. He looked down. He could now see the lifeless form towards the edge of the pool to his side. He dived again and, this time, managed to grab hold of the child's leg. With difficulty, he surfaced. Baywatch, this was not, but eventually, the child was grabbed and pulled out of the pool. It was difficult to decide who needed resuscitation first. Dave got out of the pool and then turned around and retched back into it. Fortunately, it was still happy hour.

Rhiannon had now joined the small group of guests, and Dave realised that the boy was still not breathing. He wiped some vomit from his mouth and knelt by the lifeless child. And then miraculously, from somewhere deep within him, a sober competent anaesthetist took over. He shouted to Rhiannon, to get an ambulance. Then commanded them not to go near the broken light. He cleared the child's airway. Thumped him on the chest for good luck, and then commenced a series of compressions, interspersed with breaths delivered via mouth to mouth.

Nothing. He continued for two minutes; still nothing. "Do you have a defibrillator?" he asked the hotel manager, who had now joined the group. He gestured two paddles and a jolt of electricity. The manager looked terrified and shook his head. Dave's brain whirred. The child had suffered an initial electric shock followed by drowning. He looked about eight.

Rhiannon was now by his side, looking very surprised to see him. He turned to her.

"Hi, gorgeous. I need a couple of large dry towels. And check if any of the hotels have a defib. We need one pronto." He continued with the chest compressions and artificial breathing.

A crowd had now gathered around the group. The child's parents were still nowhere to be seen. A siren wailed in the distance. Every minute seemed an age, and Dave realised that the longer the child's heart was stopped, the lower the likelihood that he would have any chance of recovering.

Towels arrived. "Dry him and then put him on a dry towel," he ordered.

A paramedic team arrived at the far end of the pool. They looked in panic at the child.

"Defibrillator," said Dave. "Electricity!" He mimicked someone being electrocuted. A machine was brought over. Dave applied the paddles to the child's chest and side. It was an adult machine, and he prayed that it wouldn't fry the kid's heart. "Stand back," he ordered. The machine whirred and charged. He could see the zigzagging shockable rhythm on its screen. He pressed the button, and life stood still. Life literally stood still.

Dave could clearly see the frightened faces around him. The dead child. The pool, the sun, Rhiannon looking desperately at him. His vomit in the pool. It was all in slow motion. He looked down at the pale child. Come on son, he thought. You don't deserve to die. Even though you're a little sod. There was a jolt.

And that was it. Miraculously, the child's pulse returned, along with the colour to his lips. The young body recovered astonishingly rapidly. There was a gasp from the onlookers. Ratboy opened his startled eyes wide, looked at Dave, still wearing the yellow luminous goggles and promptly attempted to punch him in the face. He then coughed hard and tried to get up. Meanwhile, his parents had now joined the throng.

"What the fuck have you done to my son, you pervert?" screamed his mother.

Dave tried to stand up. He looked awful. Sodden clothes, ruined shoes and his hair stuck to his face. The goggles made him look like a deranged wasp.

"He just saved your son's life, you stupid cow," replied Rhiannon. And then she moved across, embraced Dave, and kissed him full on the mouth. "You are my hero," she added, "which is good as I think I have just been sacked. And you smell of sick."

A spontaneous round of applause and relieved cheers followed. The child was taken away in the ambulance and the crowd gradually dispersed. The relieved looking manager came over and offered him a glass of brandy.

"*Fantastico!*" he said. "I thought the boy dead!"

"I think you need to fix the pool light," replied Dave with a smile.

"Si, Si. Gracias Señor."

"I'd better get back to the kids," Rhiannon said. "Thank you. Meet me after work. Six o'clock. I'm taking you out." She smiled and turned. Dave simply stood. His mouth opened and closed wordlessly. His heart was beating fast. And he could feel the palpitations. I think I might need that bloody defibrillator too, he thought as he necked the brandy in one.

*

At an airport approximately eight miles away, a budget airline had just landed. One of its recently disembarked occupants was now in the bathroom. A profuse bout of diarrhoea had at least settled some of his abdominal colic. His shirt was drenched in sweat, and he looked ghastly. He held his pale, thin face in his hands and inwardly cursed his boss. He loathed flying. After eventually emerging from the cubicle, he walked over to the basin and winced at his reflection. Narcissus himself would have baulked. He splashed cold water over his face and surveyed his sweat-sodden shirt with dismay. A text came through. *ARE YOU THERE YET?* He sent a curt *YES* in reply and reached into his bag to get the instructions that had been provided for him. *GO TO THE BUS STOP OUTSIDE THE TERMINAL AND GET BUS FORTY TO LOS CRISTIANOS.*

Myles looked longingly at the taxi rank. Quicker. Direct. He hated his boss almost as much as he hated flying. He dripped with more sweat. Fifteen minutes later, the bus arrived, and he was pleasantly surprised by how cool it was. He had a mobile map app on his phone and could at least track his progress to the El Ole Hotel and apartment complex, where he was booked to stay.

Armed with three photographs of his targets along with brief additional details of their lives, he had a suitcase, a company credit card, and a small bottle of water. He could feel the pink skin on his forehead beginning to burn. As the bus sped down the motorway towards its destination, he thought about his mission. What did he know about these three doctors? He knew that his boss wanted him to dig up as much dirt as possible on them. He'd read the files. And the newspaper extracts.

He knew about Tom's explosive antics in the crematorium, Sid's prescription for priapism and Dave's unintended CCTV appearance. What disquieted him, however, were the other snippets that he knew. He knew that Tom had run a difficult urban practice in Doncaster, an impoverished Yorkshire town with high levels of deprivation, and had suffered from depression and alcohol problems as a result. He knew that Sid had received a commendation for his outstanding contribution to general practice a few years earlier, despite significant institutional prejudice. Even more uncomfortably, he was aware that Dr Dave was considered one of the best anaesthetists in the northern region, despite his sexual antics. He also knew that his boss at the RMC was focussed on getting his name in the New Year's honours list and was colluding with the minister of health to further their mutual careers.

Myles was timid and easily bullied into submission, but he retained some sense of decency and an awareness of core values, unlike his boss, who seemed to have traded his soul a long time ago. He has a sense of discomfort that he may be fighting on the wrong side of this war. Born into a middle-class family, he had been sent to a struggling state school 'to toughen him up' and had been bullied relentlessly for his effeminate ways and slight stature. He knew that his parents, especially his father, would never accept his sexuality, and so he had drifted between jobs after finishing an English degree, ending up in the RMC.

He looked at his clothes and shoes. They were ruined. He took a hesitant sniff of one armpit and recoiled. He slumped miserably back in his chair. His phone buzzed again. *WTF RU?* As he gazed out of the window, the arid landscape rushed past him. He sighed and picked up his phone. *ON A BUS TO THE*

HOTEL YOU MISERABLE ABOMINATION OF A HUMAN BEING he typed. He thought better of the last seven words, deleted them, and pressed send.

ABOUT BLOODY TIME came the reply. *KEEP YOUR HEAD DOWN AND REPORT BACK AS SOON AS YOU FIND THEM.* He simply replied, *OK*. A few minutes later, and as the sun was starting to set, he arrived at his hotel. At the main desk, a man was shouting at the concierge.

"It's a bloody disgrace. I'll see you Dagos in court. What are you going to do about it? Eh? Do you speak English or what?"

Myles stood back, but the man turned around. "Tried to bloody murder my kid they did," he said loudly to anyone within earshot, which would have covered a significant distance. Myles smiled politely.

"Good job, you had a doc here, or he'd be dead now. Bloody disgrace," continued the other guest. "I demand you move us to a decent hotel. If he survives, that is. And I don't expect to get a bill neither."

Myles was now alert. "That sounds, erm, terrible," he said. "What happened to your, er, son?"

"Well 'e's a bit hyper. Good kid mind. But he don't just like doing one fing. Playing 'armlessly and then bang!" He threw his arms in the air. Myles recoiled. "Then nearly drowns. At a bleedin' kids club too. Stupid cow wasn't looking after 'em proper. Bloody disgrace."

"Do you mean his mother?" asked Myles.

The man looked incredulous. "No, the 'oliday rep!"

"Ah, of course. And the person who helped you?" enquired Myles quickly, anxious not to antagonise the bull further.

"Bloody 'ero. English doc, I think. Dived in and brung 'im round. Best docs 'em NHS ones. Makes you proud."

"Did you catch his name, was he, um, of colour?"

"He looked a bit sunburnt, but I told you 'e was English. Tall lad. Kept pretty cool considering."

"Was there anyone else there?" asked Myles.

"Well, I didn't get there for a bit cos we was in the bar, but I fink 'e sorted it by 'imself. Even when the ambulance come and took our kid away. Wife's with 'im now. Poor little bastard."

If the mother was anything like the father, Myles certainly felt sorry for the 'poor little bastard'.

"Well, I hope he recovers very soon." Myles decided it best to come back for his room key a little later. He stifled an involuntary shudder and turned away.

"Yeah, fanks."

Meanwhile, the man turned back to the cowering receptionist and restarted his tirade. A few decibels louder this time to facilitate any language barrier. Myles walked quietly into the bar area. And promptly walked back out. His boss had clearly no regard for his wellbeing. The Hotel El Ole was aptly named, he thought.

Across the road, Myles' arrival had been noticed by Dave, who had downed another couple of beers to settle his nerves after the incident. Dave, of course, had never seen Myles before, but he recognised a freshly arrived guest. He had left the bar shortly before Ratboy's father, or rather stepfather, had commenced his tirade at the hotel desk and had been about to head back to his own hotel to be ready to meet Rhiannon for dinner when the prospect of another happy hour had seduced him.

He was clearly shaken. A resuscitation, in the sterile confines of a hospital, wouldn't have phased him one bit. He'd done hundreds. Maybe even a thousand. But this one seemed more human. More raw. More chaotic. He knew he would have been unsafe to drive a car after that amount of beer and wondered what the headlines might have been, had the attempt failed. The vomit cocktail in the pool was mainly due to the pool water, but the alcohol was also a factor. With a slice of luck and a twist of fate for decoration.

It had really hit him when he'd sat down afterwards. He had felt scared for the first time in his medical career. Vulnerable. Fallible. He had nursed the remnants of his second happy hour beer for the last ten minutes and was about to gulp it down when he saw Myles standing at the bar. He looked out of place - an executive type; briefcase, pallid skin, wholly inappropriate clothes and shoes for a holiday resort and no one else with him. He hadn't seen a more miserable or unlikely looking sun-seeker in a long time. Dave retreated a little further back into the shadows in the corner.

The man at the bar was now trying to get the attention of the barman, who was watching the football on the TV on the wall.

"Excuse me," he said. "Pardon me but could I...?"

The barman looked over quizzically. "*Señor?*"

"Um a gin and tonic please. And a glass of water."

"Ice, *Señor?*"

Go careful with the ice here, thought Dave. Unless you've brought triple-ply toilet paper with you.

"Ah, yes. Please." Two gin and tonics were brought. Large ones. Myles looked puzzled.

"Two for one, *Señor,*" the barman smiled and pointed at the sign on the wall and the clock next to it. He then turned back to the football. "Pay when finish." He added as an afterthought over his shoulder.

Dave looked at his watch. Five o'clock. He really needed to leave, but he hadn't paid for his beers, and he had the feeling that this city dweller wasn't in Tenerife for the sunshine. He was fascinated. He thought quickly. Dave looked very scruffy: still in the same sodden shoes from earlier and still-damp shirt and shorts. He also had his cap, which he now put on his head. The shades would look ridiculous at this time of night. Fortunately, he hadn't kept his phone in his pocket during his unplanned sub-aqua adventure, but his wallet was sodden.

He waited until Myles appeared to be on his own phone, teetered a little drunkenly to the bar, left a ten Euro note on the counter and muttered, "*Buenos noches, Pablo,*" in a thick accent which was made more comical by the fact that it was still early evening, and the barman was called Eloy. Nevertheless, Eloy picked up the eight euro tip, shrugged his shoulders and turned back to the football. He'd been called worse. Myles was still trying to get reception on his phone. Dave continued down the road and walked the short distance to his own hotel. He felt for his key card. Sod it. He bet it was still in the bottom of the pool. Great. It was white too. Nicely camouflaged against the pool floor. He looked at his watch. Odd. Still only five. Then he looked at the clock in the wall of the bar. Quarter past six.

"Oh bollocks. I'm late.". His watch face beamed back at him. A fixed grin. Water had bound its mechanism useless. He grabbed some of the flowers from a nearby table and started to run. His shoes squelched rhythmically as he did so, and a group of teenage girls giggled as he passed them.

"Run Forrest, run!" one called after him in encouragement.

Dave's heart pounded. His head pounded. His feet pounded. All he could think of was that she wouldn't be waiting for him. For the first time in his life, something really mattered to him. The alcohol was now hitting his brain. He darted around a corner, almost colliding with a mobility scooter and incumbent, travelling in the opposite direction. He narrowly avoided a loose kerb. Finally, he could see the hotel lights in the distance. A neon Mecca beckoned him. His chest ached. His eyes watered. His feet blistered.

And there she was. Standing just by the palm tree at the side of the entrance. In dark blue jeans and a white silk top. Simple but stunningly effective. He slowed to a brisk, ungainly jog. He looked down at himself. His outfit would have made a charity shop mannequin wince. His hair was flattened against his head, making him look like a cross between Oliver Hardy and Adolf Hitler. On bad hair days.

And then she saw him too. He had now stopped. Unsure whether to run towards her or hide in the nearest bush. Her mouth opened and closed silently. And then she beamed and ran towards him.

"Dave, you look… you look…" she laughed. "You look the most human I've ever seen you." She put her arms around him, kissed him and added, "And you've never smelt more manly."

This time they both laughed.

"So shall we just head out like this then?" he asked.

One look at her expression suggested that a shave and a shower, followed by clean clothes, were a minimum prerequisite still.

"And put on some of this," she added. "But just a little."

She handed him a small bottle of aftershave called 'Hero'. She smiled at him. He smiled back. He felt overwhelmed by a sudden desire to tell her how he felt about her, but as they stood together, gazing into each other's eyes, holding each other's hands, he sensed that words were unnecessary.

*

Meanwhile, at an airport in Southern Turkey, a smart, focused looking Indian lady was passing very slowly through passport control, heading towards the last place that she had picked up her soon-to-be ex-husband's, phone signal. A pretty flight attendant smiled pleasantly at her as she walked past the long queue on her way to her airline desk, ready for her next trip to Lisbon. The second phone in her bag switched to flight only mode.

CHAPTER FOURTEEN: READ ALL ABOUT IT

Manchester

The headline writer had had a creative day. 'Doc doc, dash dash dash!' the headline screamed from the front page of Tom's least favourite tabloid newspaper. Underneath this were photos of the three of them, alongside a photo of a younger-looking Lexy, wearing lingerie and standing astride a motorbike. Full story page four. A lesser story about some avoidable killer disease in a famine-affected region somewhere 'in Africa', was initially squashed into a small gap at the bottom of the page and then moved to page seven to allow more space for the photo of Lexy.

"Let's be honest," the editor had said. "Who gives a shit about dying Africans when you can gawp at a fit bird in suspenders on a Harley?!"

His nearly one million readers no doubt agreed with him.

Sid's photograph had been taken straight from a medical conference showing him standing next to a 'Viagra' stand. (The original stand had been for a new anti-malarial drug but had been photoshopped). Dave's showed him drunk with each arm around a giggling student nurse, each wearing bunny ears at a fancy dress party. Admittedly, this was genuine. Meanwhile, Tom's facial colour had been changed to yellow to make him appear jaundiced. A half-empty bottle of whiskey added to the frame for effect.

Tom looked at the newspaper sitting in the stand, and was gripped initially with shock, followed rapidly by anger. And followed shortly after that by fear. He bought a copy, a first for him. Then a second for the others. He texted Sid. *SEEN THE PAPERS THIS MORNING?* Sid had, unfortunately. *I NEVER EVEN BLOODY WELL DRANK WHISKY*, he added. *WHEN SHOULD WE MEET UP?*

GOT COIN COLLECTION replied Sid. *INDIAN PASSPOTT* (texting never was his strength) *AND SPARE CREDIT CARD. NOTHING LEFT HERE FIT ME.* Tom got the gist.

MANCHESTER PICCADILLY STATION. PUB 200 YARDS TOWARDS THE GARDENS. GREASYSPOONS ON RIGHT. 4PM. Tom thought for a moment. He was stressed. He hadn't had a drink in a month, and although he hadn't missed it much so far, the newspaper article had rekindled an old fear that the cycle could restart. He knew his liver may not survive many more rounds. He texted again. *SORRY, SEE YOU AT THE COFFEE PLACE JUST PAST IT. SAME TIME. BIG BUCKS.* At the other end of the line, Sid breathed a sigh of relief for his friend.

Lexy, with horror, had also seen the headline. She seethed. How on earth had they managed to get hold of that photo, taken years ago, by her ex-boyfriend who had subsequently run off with her roommate? She wasn't sure who to hate more. Her ex, the newspaper, or the newspaper readers. It felt such an invasion of her privacy. She felt like she had been raped. Again. The article itself was mainly about the three doctors, disgraced by the RMC and now on the run, probably in the Canary Islands. Abetted by Lexy, a barmaid from a London bar (she had been the bloody acting manager, she murmured to herself indignantly). They had allegedly stolen their confidential reports from the RMC, along with other health service sensitive information, and fled the country.

A detailed account of the contents of the confidential reports relating to Sid, Dave and Tom were then given, with a few salacious details added to maintain the reader's pique. Their salaries had been estimated and then doubled for good measure, to amplify their readers' indignation. The head of the RMC had expressed dismay at the reckless actions of the doctors, whilst the Secretary of State for Health had added: 'this is a sorry state of affairs for the NHS, reflecting a general decline in standards of doctors' behaviour. The Government has a duty of care to protect vulnerable patients and will work hard, alongside the RMC, to explore every possible alternative to the current system, which is clearly failing. The previous Government's failed attempted reforms have not helped'.

The newspaper correspondent added that it was 'an absolute disgrace that doctors were being allowed to exploit and misuse the NHS's scant resources for their own benefit and abuse the trust of the taxpaying public. Bevin would turn in his grave' it added, speculatively. It was almost although the article had been anticipated and pre-written. On the next page was a full-page advert for private health insurance. A topless photo of a celebrity, taken with a long-distance lens, had displaced the famine article back to page seven.

It was heartfelt, earnest, and of course, utter crap, thought Lexy. Ground bait for the gullible. Designed to tempt their readers towards the main baited hook. In the short time she had known the Crash Team, she had learnt a lot about them. Lexy was intuitive, observant and a good judge of character. Having worked in pubs and bars for many years, she could usually suss a personality type out within a minute or so. She called this her 'inbuilt creepyometer' which was alerted when someone gave her the creeps for no obvious reason. It was non-specific, lacked any scientific basis and unerringly accurate. The man from the RMC has sent it off the Richter scale almost immediately.

She could easily spot the flaws in all three founder members of the Crash Team. They were all varying shades of inadequate and under-confident, but also transparent. Two showed addictive traits. But all three shared the same basic values of decency. Money didn't seem a primary motivator for any of them. They cared. They wanted to help people. They fretted. And their careers had simultaneously and spectacularly divebombed in a way that would have shamed an Olympic synchronised high board team. Sid had the lowest creepyometer score. Tom barely registered a one. Maybe a two. Whilst Dave got a superficial seven, a figure which fell the longer you knew him.

Investment bankers usually set her alarm bells off, although they were very much of a 'type'. She could usually repel them with a sharp retort, followed by a deliberate spillage if required. Their narcissistic traits were fairly uniform, if irritating, but fairly easily handled. She assumed that to make serious money at the expense of others required a clinical ability to bypass the ethical centres in the brain. It was probably a prerequisite characteristic, however objectionable. Better still, have no ethical centre at all.

The health minister's appearance at The Wolf and Whistle, however, had caused her the most disquiet. She couldn't quite work out why. He was superficially charming, polite and hadn't shown an over-enthusiastic interest in her cleavage. He spoke with a privately educated accent. Crisp. Clear. Self-Confident. Little different from the many professional men who had passed through the bar. But something about him was different. More sinister. She imagined that he could have been a silent assassin. Disappearing, smiling, back into the throng of a dinner party after calmly disposing of the host.

Initially, she couldn't work out his motive for meeting the RMC chairman either. She had sensed a degree of dislike, even disdain that he incompletely disguised, not only for the man, but also for the venue. She had heard snippets of their conversation, which clearly hadn't been intended for wider ears. His voice had been quiet but insistent. Calm but threatening. He also covered his mouth when speaking, which had made it very difficult for her to lip read the conversation. He had noticed her watching them both, and his brief glance had been icy, threatening, and dangerous.

Lexy looked back at her copy of the paper. She had already discovered that what she had stumbled across in the bag left in her pub had been more significant than just the medical records of three doctors. In fact, she suspected that the doctors were being set up as a deliberate decoy. But to get onto the front page of a national tabloid hinted at a degree of desperation for whoever wanted the information back. And also, influence from a senior source.

"Bloody doctors, eh? Never trust em, me!" The voice was that of the newsagent who had sold her the paper. "Pretty girl, though." He smiled at her. She turned and walked away quickly, hoping that he hadn't recognised her from her photo, grainy though it was. Her phone showed a text from Sid. *HOPE YOU ARE OK. SO SORRY YOU'RE DRUGGED INTO THIS. MEETING TOM LATER. PLEASE PHONE WHEN FREE. KR. R XX*

She smiled at his misspelling. She replied. *I'M FINE. WILL*

DO XX. She wasn't fine. She knew full well that it was only a matter of time before somebody in the pub disclosed more juicy details about her to the press. She still needed to pick up her notes for her book and her meagre savings. She couldn't risk being recognised by her regulars, and her only remaining option was to contact Meg, the other cleaner. Firstly though, it was time for a makeover. Her long, jet black locks had been her trademark for more than a decade, but it was time for a change. She decided to opt for a dramatic new look. Shorter, blonder, and curlier. She couldn't risk going into a salon, but she knew just who to ask. She looked for the number in her phone's directory, crossing her fingers as she did so. It was still under 'F' for funeral directors.

CHAPTER FIFTEEN: IT STARTS WITH 'FUN'

"Oh my god, darling. I'm so sorry. How intrusive. I read all about it in the paper…"

Graham stopped himself and looked briefly embarrassed as he tried to hide his copy. "Are you ok. Can I help at all?" Graham was dressed in a white tunic, resplendent with a surgical mask and bright blue gloves. He smelt of formalin.

"Yes, you can. I need you to change my hair. Completely."

Graham looked at her, tilting his head to one side. "Are we talking a trim and tint or a total transformation, darling? Marilyn Manson or Monroe?"

"The second one," said Lexy.

Graham held his hands to his face. "Oh my god. I'm so excited. Could I ask one thing, though?"

"I'm skint if that's what you mean," replied Lexy.

"No, no, all I meant was could you lie flat as I'm doing it. I'm not used to…"

"Cutting the hair of the living," Lexy finished helpfully.

"Well, I'm more coffin coiffure than salon savvy," he added. "Sorry darling, but your own mother won't recognise you."

"That would be a challenge," murmured Lexy to herself. Her adoptive mother was dead, and her own mother hadn't seen her since childhood.

"I've got one more corpse, erm, one more client left. Then I'll just erm have a clean-up and be with you, darling." Lexy shuddered but smiled thinly back at him. "And you have to tell me all about your life since I last saw you! Is it five years?"

"Eight," corrected Lexy.

Eight years previously, Lexy had worked at the funeral directors in South East London where Graham had also worked. M Barnum and Son Ltd. At the interview, the manager had taken one look at her (two to be honest, the second as she left his office) and offered her a position on the reception desk. "You're exactly what I'm looking for," he'd said. He thought that she looked like a young Morticia from the Adams family, seemed articulate, and he hoped her body might offer a more animated viewing in the quiet room than was usual.

He'd been disappointed when the only developing stiffness in the place had remained the rigor mortis of the incumbent guests. A year later, she had been dismissed on some feeble grounds, but had learnt a lot in the process and genuinely been good at her job. She'd also helped herself to some of the 'ash cash' which had been prepared for the following week's doctors when they completed the cremation forms. She still felt rather guilty about this but knew she wouldn't receive her final month's pay and needed to pay her rent.

Graham was openly gay. Proud of it, extremely camp and great fun, at least when sober. He could turn a road crash victim into a pageant princess, which was usually of huge comfort to the bereaved families, with the notable exception of one, when he inadvertently changed the sex of the victim. "Darling, he looked much better as a girl," Lexy had remembered him pleading at his subsequent disciplinary meeting.

"Most of my clients look better now they're dead than they ever did alive," was his standard, and not unsubstantiated, boast.

He had collected a few secret tools of the trade over the years, including gaffer tape, safety pins and staples, but these were usually hidden, beautifully discretely. An hour and a half, and a long and untruthful yarn later, involving money lenders, strip clubs and the Bulgarian mafia (Graham had lapped up every word of it), Lexy emerged. Ready for her fictional trip back to Northern Europe.

She gasped as she looked in the mirror. She had to admit, he'd done a great job, including facial makeup. So much so that she barely recognised her own reflection. Graham looked immensely proud.

"May I ?" He took out his phone for a photograph.

"One, Graham, but you have to promise not to share it with anyone. There's social media in Bulgaria, too, remember!"

Graham looked suitably anxious. "Oh god, darling, of course. Of course. Mum's the word. My lips are more sealed than Melania Trump's legs since her wedding." With that, he took several shots and saved them on his phone.

She knew full well that he was the most indiscreet man she knew. He was likely to repeat the story to only a few of his equally indiscreet friends, and by the rule of exponential growth, most of the Northern Hemisphere would soon know. And Melania had borne at least one child as far as she knew.

She texted Sid. CAN GET TO MANCHESTER TONIGHT. WHERE SHALL WE MEET?

Meanwhile, Graham had texted his closest friends with a photo. OMG! YOU'LL NEVER GUESS WHO I JUST STYLED. TOP SECRET THOUGH! TELL NO ONE! G X.

Lexy looked in the mirror again. She wanted to cry. It was certainly a fabulous temporary disguise, but she looked like the Sindy doll she'd played with as a child. As soon as she was back in Tenerife, she'd have a crop cut. She guessed she had around twenty-four hours before her photo went viral. They'd then be looking for a decoy.

She was very fond of Graham, as indiscreet as he was. He'd been kind to her and once even made a bizarre, if drunken, pass at her on a staff night out, telling her 'she was the only girl who could turn him straight'. He'd had no recollection of this the following day, fortunately. The Funeral Directors Association nights out had always been legendary. Far from being stuffy and dull, she'd found them to be great company. Poorly paid, genuinely caring and very funny, they worked extremely long hours and were capable of having a great night out. They'd all danced until the early hours.

Lexy's usual type were tattooed bikers, muscular, lean, and usually with a 'lived in' face. Facial scars were an optional extra. She'd even dabbled a little with her own sex but found them to be too bitchy and possessive to cope with. Her exes tended to stalk her after they broke up too.

Unfortunately, Lexy was also the bikers' type, and had had a series of unhappy relationships in which she'd usually ended up being abused in some shape or form, and then abandoned. Her self-esteem was not high, despite her undoubted beauty combined with a sharp brain and equally sharp tongue. She still couldn't work out why she had felt so drawn to Sid when he'd first asked to borrow her phone charger in The Wolf and Whistle. He was the opposite of all those things. Kind, gentle, polite. Soft skinned! But she had also noticed that he was attracted to her too. He'd given out 'good vibes'. She suspected stray animals would approach him. Opposites, she decided. Attracting each other like the poles of magnets. And their first night together had been a revelation to her. He'd been so gentle, but their passion had been raw. She'd felt like they'd both made love properly for the first time in their lives. She'd even cried afterwards, to her absolute astonishment. They'd held each other all night afterwards, and she'd awoken with his arms still wrapped tightly around her. She'd felt both safe, and simultaneously, extremely vulnerable. But it had also felt exhilarating. Her chest felt like it was full of bubbles. Despite not knowing what she was looking for, she sensed she might have stumbled across it anyway.

She looked at her phone again. She was now walking through the East London streets towards the bus stop which would take her to the main coach station in central London. She felt self-conscious and noticed that she was attracting some unwanted attention. Some builders had wolf whistled her as she'd walked past. "Allo gorgeous, wanna help us stiffen our mortar, darlin'?" She'd stifled her natural reflex reaction to tell them to 'go and fuck themselves'. She wanted to buy a hat and become invisible but realised that it would be counterproductive to wear it too soon. She needed to be seen with this hairstyle for now. She went into a charity shop, pretended to look at thousand-piece jigsaws briefly (did anyone really buy these things?), and then walked out with a beanie hat hidden under her coat.

She made sure that she looked directly into the bus camera on the way to the coach station. She'd smiled sweetly at the bus driver, who had given her a double take when she'd got on. She hoped he hadn't noticed that she'd flashed a supermarket card at the contactless pay button, as he'd been rendered temporarily distracted as the woman behind her tried to buy a ticket from him. "Are you listening to me?" She'd boomed. A young man had also offered her his seat, to her great surprise. She'd accepted it mainly out of bewilderment.

The trip to The Wolf and Whistle had been quicker and generally simpler than she'd expected. Aside from the usual regulars, there had been no one else in the pub. Mid-afternoon was always the quietest time, and the horse racing had distracted the few who had enough energy to take any notice. She'd slipped into the bar at the rear, climbed the flight of stairs (praying she wouldn't meet anyone on the way) slipped silently into her old room and found her notes along with the small metal box. It still contained around six hundred pounds. Enough for emergencies, as pre-planned. She noticed that the rest of the room seemed to have been cleaned and emptied.

As she left the room, she heard a voice down below. "Is there any chance of getting a fackin' beer around 'ere this week?"

She smiled. Old yella was still faithfully sat at his master's chair. She was almost tempted to go down and serve him herself when she heard footsteps coming from above her.

"Alright, alright. You won't bloody dehydrate. Let a man have a shit for god's sake." This second sentence was delivered with fewer decibels than the first. She quickly hid behind the room door until her old boss had descended into the bar.

Now she felt trapped. If she stayed where she was for too long, she'd end up missing the coach north and risk being found. She'd noticed the copy of the newspaper on the main bar with a circle drawn around her photo.

"Why were men so base?" she asked herself. And then she got her chance.

"Hey, hey everyone, it's the news. Let's see if our Lexy's made national headlines yet."

She knew they'd be glued to the TV in the far corner long enough for her to slip out, hopefully still unnoticed. They'd be hoping the press had uncovered some more lurid photos that may be of interest to the public. And so she did. But not before first picking up the newspaper and carrying it out with her, ready for the nearest appropriate receptacle, marked 'no hot ashes'. She then boarded a second bus, less eventfully this time, and had finally attempted to hold a conversation with an elderly couple in the queue for tickets at Victoria Coach station. "Do you know which kiosk sells tickets to Paris?" she'd asked innocently. "I'm heading to France."

Finally she'd popped into the disabled toilet, stuffed her new golden locks under the grey beanie hat and surreptitiously bought a student ticket to Manchester. The bored looking ticket vendor hadn't given her a second glance or asked to see her non-existent student card. She sat towards the rear of the coach, put a set of earphone buds in her ears (they weren't attached to anything, but she hoped it would stop anyone speaking to her) and curled into a ball. For the first hour or so, she simply closed her eyes, but the rhythmic rocking and hum of the coach engine soon coaxed her into a deep sleep. 'Into the arms of Morpheus', as her adoptive father had told her. The Greek god of sleep.

In her dreams, she was lying on a sunbed next to a pool. It was warm and relaxing. She was reading a book and drinking a glass of something sweet. Children were playing with a ball in the distance. She imagined that she'd been there a very long time. She felt safe. Then suddenly she was on a motorcycle. Her hair flying backwards in the wind as she sped along, carefree. She had a passenger riding pillion behind her. He was holding her tightly and it felt nice. Secure. She wasn't sure who this was.

Next she was lying on a bed again, but this time it was on a slab in a funeral directors. She could smell formalin in her nostrils, and her hair was being cut and styled. She could hear Graham's voice as he tugged at her hair, but she couldn't move. She tried to scream but she was now being lifted and put into a coffin. The lid was going on. She could hear the nails being hammered in. She couldn't breathe. Suddenly there was a loud noise, and the lid was ripped off. She saw Sid's face. He put his lips to hers and breathed into her chest. She felt his warm breath fill her lungs and she relaxed. He was breathing for her. She felt a tug at her arm from the side. It wasn't Sid. She stirred.

"Hello, miss. You ok? We've arrived. In Manchester. You need to get off or you'll end up back in London." The driver looked at her kindly. "Here." He gave her a bottle of orange juice. "You look like you need this." And he helped her gather her things as she got off. "You've dropped this," he said and handed her a carrier bag of papers and her phone. She flushed with embarrassment and relief.

"Thank you," she said. "You're very kind."

He looked at her as she descended unsteadily off the bus and walked away. As she did so, she looked at her phone. Sid had texted her. She beamed with relief.

Another evacuee from London, the driver thought. Pretty girl. Odd hat to cover that beautiful hair though. He expected she'd gone there to find her fortune and found her misfortune instead. Now she was trying to remain incognito. He sighed to himself and gazed into the distance. She reminded him of someone, but he couldn't quite place her.

"Oi, Wilson, you lazy arse, liven up, sunshine!" It was his colleague from the bus company. "You coming for a fag or what? You're setting off again in thirty minutes, and traffic'll be shite." Wilson shrugged his shoulders. Trinidad, where he had spent his entire, carefree childhood, seemed so very far away nowadays.

"Of course. What a kind invitation, the highlight of my day," he replied with gentle irony. "Gotta support the Government's tax revenue and die prematurely, eh? Save 'em paying my pension?!"

"Not with mine you won't," grinned his colleague. "These 'aven't come through customs! They'll still kill you, though." Both men laughed.

*

Sid was waiting for her at the Mega Bucks coffee shop. He'd ordered her a hot chocolate and was waiting near the window, looking out for her. She walked past him three times, the final time more slowly. Finally, she stopped by his table and asked if she could clear the empty cups. He looked up, startled.

"Lexy? Oh my goodness. You. I. I'm so sorry I didn't recognise you."

"Well that's good really," she'd said and smiled.

"No need for me to change my look," he'd said. "What's another brown face in this city?" He'd said it without a hint of bitterness, but she wondered how it must have felt, coming over to work in a frequently hostile new country, all those years ago.

"Well, I'd spot your handsome face anywhere," she'd said simply. And smiled. Her own lovely face, less pale than usual following her time in Tenerife, was framed on three sides with long, artificial looking, golden tresses.

"What do you think of it?" she asked him.

Sid looked at her. He paused. "Lexy, please don't take this the wrong way, because you do look very beautiful. You always look beautiful. But would you be offended if I said I prefer your usual look. It's more… you."

Lexy beamed. He'd given the answer she'd hoped to hear. "It's temporary, I assure you," she'd said. "I hate it!" They both laughed.

"I've got you a hot chocolate, but I can get you anything else. Can I get you something to eat?"

Lexy reached for his hand. Picked it up gently. Kissed it softly on the dorsum, and then looked at his watch. "Sorry, my phone is flat this time," she said. "I'd lost all track of time. Do you possibly have a charger, young man?" At first he looked slightly worried and started to look in his bag, but she smiled at

142

him and said, "Sid, I'm teasing you." She took out her own charger and plugged it into the socket adjacent to their legs.

"Where's Tom?" she asked. "And have you heard from the others?"

"Tom said he'd meet us in an hour or so," replied Sid. "He says he needed to sort a few things out. He's really upset about the article." Sid looked around the coffee shop, but no one was taking any notice of them. He continued. "He didn't say much. Just that he had to sort out a few loose ends."

"Do you think he's started drinking again?" asked Lexy.

Sid looked at her in surprise. "How did you know about that?" he asked.

"Sid, it's obvious. I've worked in pubs for years. Some of my best friends are alcoholics! Were alcoholics." She paused. A slight wave of sadness passed over her. "I mean, some of the people I thought were my best friends were alcoholics," she said. "It turns out that their own best friends resided in bottles. Anyway, I hope not. He seems very lost still."

"There's a lot of anger and bitterness in him," replied Sid. "He misses his children in particular. Like I do. Though in his case, the relationship really seems to have broken down with them. He's lost contact. In the end, all he really had was his patients. No doubt they adored him. And then the RMC bombshell comes along and what's left for him?"

"Do you think he's lonely?" she asked.

"Lexy, I think both him and Dave are lonely. Dave fills his void with empty relationships. I'm not sure what Tom does."

"I think Dave already has a new beginning about to start," she said." He clearly likes Rhiannon, and she likes him too."

"Don't you think the age gap is a problem?" Sid asked this and looked slightly nervous as he did so.

"No, not at all," she said this emphatically. "She's older than him mentally anyway."

Sid smiled. "You're so funny," he said. "This time, he held her hand and kissed the back of it gently."

"I haven't got a watch if you're trying to check the time," she smirked back at him. He made a mental note to buy her one.

"It doesn't matter," he said. "I think time is standing still anyway."

*

Tom had given himself a stiff talking to. "You bloody miserable git," he'd said. "Stop feeling sorry for yourself." He'd looked at the reflection staring seriously back at him. The words 'MUFC 4 ever' had been added to one corner of the glass by a local wordsmith. A wit had added 'I will hate' just above this, no doubt one of the sky blue tribe from the other side of the city. The ice cold sliver of fear which had cut through his brain earlier, had morphed into a steely determination to do something. He looked at the words 'I will hate' again.

An odd thing really, he thought. Two perfectly good football teams. Two sets of near identical fans. The separation was a few hues of the rainbow spectrum on their shirts. Why not just make a team to unite a city? He looked in the mirror again. How much of his misfortune had he simply brought on himself? A desire to prove himself, following years of being bullied. An addiction to the adoration metered upon him by his grateful patients. Finding a job he was genuinely good at. A desire to avoid the poverty which had blighted his own childhood. It was a heady cocktail. A splash of this. A twist of that. Icy and cold in places with a sweet centre, but a bitter aftertaste. Pride. One of the seven deadly sins for good reason.

He had gone to the pub earlier, near Piccadilly station. He'd got to the door and was about to go in when an old homeless man had looked directly at him.

"It'll be the death of you, you know. Spare an old man some change."

Tom had looked at him. Looked at the gaunt face, into the haunted eyes and at the sallow complexion. The teeth were rotten. The cheeks sunken. He looked like death. Every vitamin deficiency you could think of, concentrated into one body. What had he been in a younger life, Tom wondered. Someone's father or husband. Maybe a teacher or even a doctor like him? Tom shuddered. He knew how many people on the street were ex-armed forces. How a few missed paycheques and a little bad luck could ruin even the most orderly of lives.

"It's not the answer you know," the man added. "Look at me. Sergeant with the Queens own, once I was. Now pissing myself in a shop doorway, begging for change."

Tom looked at him again. He was genuinely spooked. What did this man know about him?

"We were all once human too you know," the man said. "Us homeless lot. Don't run away, doc. Face the music."

And that was it, he turned back to the street. "Penny for an old man. Spare some change please. God bless you."

Tom spotted the copy of the newspaper by his side. He could see his face looking out from the front page. He knew that there were fewer differences between them than he wanted to admit. He then took the ten pound note he was going to buy his beer with.

"Here, sergeant. To your health," he said and placed the note in the old man's hand. "Thank you."

"Queen and country sir, Queen and country!" The old man smiled back. Then he winked. "I was in reconnaissance," he said proudly and turned back again to look at the many faces in the street that all looked elsewhere. Tom paused. He did still go into the pub, but mainly because he needed to empty his bladder. The toilets were upstairs for the benefit of the disabled. (Why take up valuable drinking space on the ground floor?) And as he looked into the mirror, with the inscribed words of wisdom, he vowed to clean his act up and redirect his anger towards something more positive.

He texted Sid. *SEE YOU AT 9PM. I'VE BOOKED US A FAMILY ROOM AT THE TRAVEL MOTEL NEAR THE GARDENS. BAD NIGHT'S SLEEP GUARANTEED.* And then he did something he hadn't done for years. After a trip to a nearby Turkish barber for another proper shave, he went into the main library. It had a newspaper section and a quiet area where you could use their computer and printer. He'd already asked his friend Ricky to get his car MOT'd and take it round to the storage barn. He'd also amended or stopped a number of direct debits and even bought some cards and stamps.

Ricky had obliged, without question. He was like a second brother to Tom. Outwardly a bit of a basket case, who smoked heavily, swore a lot, and rarely required more than two sentences to summarise his opinion of anyone. Yet he was also clever, loyal, and probably some way along on the autistic spectrum. He had a photographic memory, an acerbic tongue and the strongest East London accent that Tom could ever recall. He would have made the perfect loveable rogue in a soap opera. He couldn't remember how long he had known him, just that he was a true friend, albeit an eccentric one.

A brief internet search had offered Tom some political background on the minister for health, including some interesting links that he appeared to have held with private companies overseas. A search for the head of the RMC had also yielded some useful information on him too, including his political affiliations as a student, and the names of the legal companies he'd worked for after qualifying in law. Tom printed off as much as could. He had a few minutes left before the library closed and so he decided to perform a third internet search, this time on the editorial staff and ownership of the tabloid, whose front page he currently graced. Nothing obvious here, but he printed off his findings anyway and added it to the pile he was collecting. Finally, he paid the librarian for the use of the printer, stapled the pages together and went to a nearby cafe to have a hot drink and write his cards.

"Do you read many books?" The librarian asked him.

"Not really," he replied honestly.

"Hm. You should," she said. "You'll find the answers to many puzzles in between the pages of a good read."

He'd thanked her, but her words did make him think. Yes, he'd start to read more. Something light initially. Funny even.

"Maybe start with Lucky Jim," she suggested with a pleasant smile. "It's very funny and slightly dark."

"Bit like the NHS," added Tom.

The astute librarian watched him as he went out through the main door. She thought she'd recognised his face. It looked worn, but the boyhood innocence was still recognisable from the photo in the newspaper.

In the cafe, the first note he wrote was to his eldest daughter.

Hi sweetie.

Hope you're ok. I know it's been ages but don't believe everything you read in the newspapers. I'm not as bad as all that really.

Miss you so much. If you fancy a bit of sunshine, come out to see me. Hope all going well with the course. Please get in touch, usual email.

Dad xx

He then did the same for his other two children, with

personalised messages, and finally, one for his sister and brother. Apologising for missing umpteen family birthdays. Then he wrote to the funeral directors, with another, almost identical one, to the chairman of his local patient participation group.

Dear Mike / Marianne

So sorry about what happened. Hope you are ok. Think of you guys a lot. Thanks for your support and friendship over the many years. I really miss working with you.
Hope we can catch up one day for a reminisce.

All the best
Tom (Doc Lawrence)

It felt cathartic. He'd simply apologised. He'd been in the wrong, and he'd let them down. He hadn't offered any excuses for his behaviour, he'd just said 'sorry' and meant it. He remembered the advice from his indemnity organisation. 'Doctors should apologise more. People often only want to feel that you care if you get something wrong and can learn from your mistakes. A simple, prompt, genuine apology is often all that is needed to defuse a situation before it escalates. It is not a sign of weakness, but a simple act of humanity.'

He wrote one final card but left the envelope blank. Inside he'd put a cutting he'd printed from an online newspaper headline. It related to the heroic actions of a three-man reconnaissance unit in the Falklands conflict, operating way in front of the main line. He suspected that the homeless sergeant had been the leader of this small unit. As he walked back through the gardens, he felt lighter than he had in years. He posted the cards and walked past the same pub, trying to see the homeless man. When he finally found him, he was fast asleep, and so Tom lay the card by his side, along with a few things he'd bought on the way back. A sandwich baguette, a bag of Heroes chocolates, some thick socks, a large bag of peanuts and a bottle of multivitamins. The card simply said:

Take care of yourself, Sergeant.
Doctor's orders
T.

As he walked away, he even did something else he hadn't done for a very long time. He said a silent prayer for the man. Unfortunately, within three months, another unknown soldier would be added to the shameful statistics of homeless street deaths. Occupationally linked, although not officially. Tuberculosis at the post-mortem. A comment of 'old shrapnel found in the right thigh' as an afterthought. The prayer must have ended up in God's unread inbox somehow.

CHAPTER SIXTEEN: SANTA'S COMING

It was Christmas Day on the maternity unit. Tom had worked since 5pm the afternoon before. His wife had tried to make the afternoon a special treat for him and their three young children, and they'd opened some of their presents together before he'd started his forty-eight-hour shift. It had been a mixed afternoon. Lovely to spend time with the children, watching their excited faces as they ripped off the wrapping paper. They'd had an early Christmas dinner a day early, but he still felt that he was missing out on sharing their childhoods and knew only too well that they would soon grow up.

He'd forgotten to bring a spare pair of socks but had learnt that the small microwave oven in his on-call room, enabled a quick dry after a prior wash of them in surgical hand scrub. The secret was to avoid washing them in the hand basin for too long, to stop the colours bleaching too much.

The wards were relatively quiet. No one wanted to stay in

hospital over Christmas, except the elderly. And as this was a maternity ward, that was unlikely. His role was to be present at the deliveries and resuscitate any babies which got into difficulties. The role required a cool head, a steady hand, and an ability to thread a small tube through a tiny gap. Either into a blood vessel or an airway. They'd asked him to be Father Christmas on the post-natal unit, and so he'd donned the requisite red suit and cotton wool beard. One of the midwives, Maria, had offered to be his special little helper when her shift ended, and then giggled with her friends as he'd blushed redder than his cloak. Worse still, he'd been tempted to say yes.

An emergency caesarean section had curtailed Santa's ward round. A prolapsed umbilical cord, threatening to cut off the blood supply to the baby before it was born. The arrest bleep had sounded, piercing the peaceful calm of the Christmas morning and he'd run in full Santa garb to the delivery suite; beard flowing as he did so. The terrified young mother had sensed the alarm amongst the staff as they'd all physically run alongside her bed, pushing her into the maternity operating theatre. The midwife was kneeling on the end of the bed precariously, with her hand physically trying to push the crown of the baby's head back, relieving the pressure on the vital blood vessels within the twisted skipping rope that protruded.

"Am I going to lose my baby?" she'd asked pleadingly as they finally got to the anaesthetic room.

He'd remembered holding her hand, pulling down his beard so that she could see his face, and looking directly into her eyes. He also remembered telling her that he'd never lost a baby through a cord prolapse yet and had no intention of making hers the first. He'd hoped he'd said this with confidence. It was also true. His only omission being that he'd never encountered a cord prolapse before in his life either. The anaesthetist was sweating through his surgical cap.

Tom looked at him. "General, I presume?" he'd asked.

"Yep, no time for a spinal," came the short reply.

The anaesthetist turned around to his ODA colleague, who looked equally anxious. "Make sure we've got two units of O Neg warming up. I hope she's not eaten much for breakfast," he muttered to himself. "Pressure on the cricoid please, Kev". The tube, mercifully, glided into her trachea in one deft movement. Tom shuddered as a lightning bolt pierced his memory.

"Right, showtime," the anaesthetist said with an attempt at calming his colleagues. Tom had stripped back to his theatre blues. There was little time to pre-warn his boss, who'd be on the other side of the city anyway, but he asked the student nurse to tell her she was needed. He thought quickly. The baby would have lost much of its vital blood oxygen in the few minutes since the cord had come down ahead of the baby's head. The midwife had reacted quickly, immediately sent out a crash call, and then attempted to stop the mother's natural desire to push. If the placenta had started to shear away from the uterus, the baby would have lost blood too.

"Peter, can you make sure they give me a long bit of cord, baby side of the clamp please?" He said this with a surreal calmness to the anaesthetist. "I need a natural hosepipe full. Can I borrow Kev too when you're finished with him?"

Peter, the ever calm, ever competent anaesthetist, nodded back. "Course. He's useless anyway!" Kev, of course, was anything but. Trench humour, though.

The Nigerian surgeon, the best Tom had seen at his craft, incised the lower skin before the iodine scrub was barely dry. He knew the urgency of getting the baby out as quickly as possible. Tom was now stood at the baby resuscitaire. Overhead heater on. Cannula and endotracheal tubes by his right hand. Suction on.

"Mec!" sounded the midwife. "Oh God, absolutely loads of it." There was a loud plop followed by a splash, and in different circumstances, the scene would have been comical. The pale green baby that emerged looked something halfway between a scrawny chicken and an alien.

"It looks dead," said the midwife, in horror.

"Long cord," reminded Tom. The green alien-chicken was brought to him, wrapped in a white towel covered in green slime and blood. Tom listened briefly for a heartbeat. "Apgar score one at one minute," he called out. "Fuck." He muttered to himself. He could hear a very slow, faint pulse only.

Kev was now stood by his side. "Bag and mask yet?"

"Not yet. Hold this up please." He handed him the length of umbilical cord. "It's our transfusion," he explained. "Let the blood run in, then clip it with this but leave me about three inches please."

"Sure no bag and mask yet, boss?"

"Not quite yet. There's still too much mec down there." Tom picked up the tiny laryngoscope. "I'll have a three point five ET and the letter 'A', though please Bob."

Clive laughed briefly. He gave him the tiny breathing tube. "Are you going to vent him?"

"Not yet. And I'll need four more of these tubes yet. We need suction first. Proper suction, or we'll drown this poor little bugger. These little fiddly suction tubes are absolute shite. Poiseuille's law and all that," he added. Tom now disconnected the main suction tube from the tiny tube connected to it. He passed the endotracheal tube through the flaccid triangle in between the lifeless vocal cords, hand-fed the suction port directly onto the end if it and then gently pulled both back in one slow, choreographed movement. There was a sickening splutter of green meconium up the tube.

"Yum, baby poo," said Tom to the ODA. "Can't really

blame it, can you. Sterile but really bloody irritating on the lungs."

"I think I've shit myself, never mind him," said Kev. The humour eased the tension.

"Right. Same again," said Tom.

"Apgar score at three minutes?" asked the midwife.

"One," said Tom and the ODA simultaneously.

Two further rapid direct suctions later and Tom said, "Right! Bag and mask now." The lifeless chest ascended and descended rhythmically. "Ten of these then I need you to compress his chest." He showed him his index and middle fingers. "Like this and the same speed. Not too hard."

Tom continued to hand ventilate the baby. Kev pressed the breastbone down rhythmically, as requested. Tom was very relieved to have Kev by his side. There was a slight colour change to blue.

"Happier alien-baby," said Tom. "Keep going."

Gradually the little body changed colour to pink.

"Stop for a second," said Tom. He put the stethoscope on the chest. "Good, we have a decent heartbeat."

"One final tube for good luck." He looked down the airway. No pea soup met his eye. "Excellent, this one's staying in!" He passed the tube again. This time there was a flicker of reaction from the baby. "This one needs taping in. Can you cut it. Just here." He indicated with his finger where to shorten the tube at the point once he was sure that both sides of the chest were inflating.

Three more minutes passed. The baby was now bright pink. The pulse rate was up. The chest was inflating on both sides. No crackles could be heard. The meconium hadn't gone too far down the lungs, thank god. Two little hands rose slightly in protest. The face grimaced. The eyes squeezed tight. Tom and Kev looked at each other.

"I think he's bloody annoyed with you," said Kev with obvious relief.

"I hope so," said Tom. He continued to ventilate a little longer and then gently pulled the tube out. There was a little whimper, gradually increasing into a steady but lusty cry.

"Apgar at ten minutes?"

"I'm going to give him an eight," said Tom. "He opened his eyes and saw Kev. Can't stop crying now."

"You cheeky bastard," laughed Clive.

"Better put him on Scooby Doo, though. They're tough little buggers these babies, but he'll need an eye keeping on him."

"It's a 'her' actually," said the midwife, who was stood nearby.

"No wonder she's crying then," said Tom. "She'll think Kev's her mother. Could I have a couple of fresh towels please? One for me and one for the baby."

He grinned across at Mike, the surgeon. "Nice one Mike," he said. Mike smiled back. "Teamwork, my friend."

They changed the towels. The midwife now came fully over to see the baby and burst into tears with relief. "I thought she was dead," she said.

"She would have been without your hand in the right place," said Tom. "Well spotted".

The SCBU staff came in with a portable incubator. Tom smiled at Claire, who was always the consummate professional.

"Ah, she's gorgeous," she said.

"They're going to call her Kevin, after her mother," said Tom. Kev towel-whipped Tom.

And so ended Christmas morning. Emma Louise (not Kevin) was feeding within two hours and sent back to the main post-natal ward. Beryl the auxiliary, spent a full hour cleaning the green slime and blood from the theatre floor.

Tom walked into the shower in his on-call room. He left his ruined theatre blues on the floor, he turned the shower on full and stood in the powerful jets of warm water for a few minutes. He felt exhausted and elated. Adrenaline was still pumping around his body. He didn't hear the gentle knock on the door but the next moment, Maria was stood, watching him.

"Hey, Santa. Hear you've been a good boy," she said. "I've brought you a towel and some fresh blues," she added. Then she paused. She smiled. And without a further word she closed the on-call room door behind her with her foot and lifted her theatre blue top over her head. She stepped out of her loose theatre trouser bottoms. Tom's mouth fell open. A perfect body was exposed to him, save for a small black underwired bra with matching thong. "Move over," she said. "Hope you don't mind, but I've unwrapped most of your Christmas present already for you, doctor."

And with that she unclipped her bra, shimmied her thong down her smooth thighs, stepped into the shower and wrapped her naked body around him.

*

When he looked back at that moment of madness, which was never repeated, he liked to think he had protested, but in reality, he only remembered three things. The overwhelming, instant lust that had consumed him, the sheer ecstasy of their final climax and the weight of the guilt that had followed for the years that followed.

Chapter Seventeen: Extra Pillows

"Now then Sid." It was Tom. He sat down with a thump at the table. Then he saw Lexy. "Holy shit!"

"Lexy is a little self-conscious about her new hairstyle," said Sid, protectively.

"It's temporary!" exclaimed Lexy.

"It's very… It's very um… Different."

"You think I look like a prostitute," said Lexy.

Tom stifled a distant memory. "No, no. Not at all. It's just very. Very different from your usual look."

"Do you think people will still recognise me from the photo in the paper?"

Not unless you're wearing lingerie at the time, he thought. Fortunately, his frontal lobe intervened before the message reached his mouth.

"Not at all," he said, but he could feel his cheeks reddening. He quickly changed the subject. "Look. I've booked accommodation tonight at the lodge. I'm afraid it's a family room. I wasn't expecting you tonight, Lexy. We'll need to check in."

"I think I can look after myself, thank you," replied Lexy. "As long as you don't both snore." Tom pulled a face. He knew he did.

"I'm so sorry, do I?" asked Sid without thinking. Lexy rolled her eyes in response.

"It's alright, Lexy, I'd guessed already," said Tom aloud, whilst thinking 'you lucky bastard', inwardly. Lexy was just his type too. Clever, slim, beautiful, and with a smoking but understated, raw sensuality.

"And we'll need a credit or debit card to check in," he added after a minor delay. "They don't allow cash anymore." He grimaced as soon as he had said this.

She looked at their expressions. A flicker of guilt ran across Tom's features. To her relief, Sid's expression was unchanged. Her eyes narrowed a fraction. I used to run a pub, remember, she thought indignantly! She looked at Sid and brushed her hair to one side as she did so. Tom smiled at this subtle sign of affection.

"Right. Plan A," he said. "We try to get a decent night's kip if we can. Then we need to look through these notes I made at the library. Lexy, would you mind taking a look through these when you get a minute? I think your sharper brain might notice something we'll miss."

Lexy looked back at him. What a strange mix he was. She'd noticed him blush when she'd asked him about her appearance, and although he wasn't her type at all physically, there was a genuine compassion and respectfulness in there too. It was particularly evident when he was in Sid's company. Sid brought out the best in him. He brought out the best in her too. Sid paid the bill and they walked across the darkening Piccadilly Gardens. Tom a fraction in front. Sid felt for Lexy's hand, just as she, instinctively, felt for his. They glanced at each other in surprise, and both reddened like teenagers, camouflaged by the dusk.

Tom beckoned the others to stay in the foyer, as he went to the desk. "Family room please. One night booked for Lawrence." The receptionist looked across at the other two and shrugged. "There's only two of you on the booking form, sir," she said. "You and your... brother." Tom looked at her.

"My sister is in town too," he added unconvincingly.

"I'll just need her name then please. Fire regulations."

Tom hesitated. "Ricky. Ricky Lawrence." He smiled back with a forced smile.

"Twenty pounds for any extra pillows," she replied with an unflinching smile. "Cash will be fine."

Tom paused and thought. "I think you've got our family name spelt wrong on your computer; would you mind correcting it please?. It's Lorenz. L-O-R-E-N-Z." He smiled and handed over the money once she had amended it and paid the rest of the bill with an infrequently used debit card. "Easily done," he added.

"Breakfast is served until half nine," she replied. "And I'd also let your bank know that they've spelt your name wrong on your card too. Easily done, eh? I recommend the full English."

Tom looked into the steely eyes. "I think we'll stick to the Continental thanks," he replied without flinching. "More variety."

Tom figured it was now a verbal-points score draw, and turned and walked back towards the others, his face set in a fixed smile.

"All ok?" asked Sid.

"Oh yes. Thatcher's Britain, alive and well still," Tom muttered in reply. And with that, the Lawrence/ Lorenz family went towards the lift which led to the furthest room on the top floor. Reserved especially for the disabled, families with small children and those with spelling errors on their bookings. For a long night of unbridled snoring. As they did, a tightly folded twenty pound note slid into a discrete purse to join the four others. Margaret liked her job. It paid well. At least this one had a sense of humour, she mused.

*

Meanwhile, a baffled new guest lay awake in her latest hotel room in Lugansk. What the hell was her bastard of a husband up to now, she fumed to herself? She doubted he could speak Ukrainian either...

*

Rhiannon and Dave were locked in a tight embrace under the soft white single bedsheet. She snored slightly, in a gentle feminine way as he held her in his arms. He looked at her sleeping face and the contour of her body. He gently stroked her hair and inhaled her soft perfume. A heady musk of Dior, light sweat and recent sexual intimacy. It smelt lovely. Familiar, yet suddenly completely new. He lay there, anticipating the usual overwhelming tidal wave of regret and desire to escape, followed by the 'one for the road' erection that usually followed. And yet all he felt was an unfamiliar contentment.

His mind wandered, and he pictured The Grinch, when he discovers that his heart has grown three sizes. He smiled at the memory of the film. "What is happening to me?" The Grinch had asked in astonishment.

Rhiannon stirred and let out a soft, contented moan. To his surprise, she reached her hand slowly down the bed, under the sheets. Dave lay guiltily still.

"Hm. I see you still love me then," she murmured and fell

back into a contented sleep.

Shit. I think I do, he thought. And despite this terrifying thought, the dreaded 'L' word, to his astonishment, his erection remained. If anything, firmer. He nuzzled into her. Kissed the nape of her neck and fell into a contented sleep himself. In his dreams, they had children, whom he carried on his shoulders. He slept with a childlike smile on his lips.

A few hundred metres away, Myles had been awoken by an incessant ringing of his phone. He didn't have to look at the number to know who it was as he answered it.

"I'm onto it, boss," he said, immediately.

"Well you'd bloody well better be," came the haughty reply. "It's me who's paying for your holiday in the sun whilst I'm back in the freezing city still."

Myles checked his phone. London was sixteen degrees. Cloudy. And he knew that the doctors of Britain were paying for his trip. "I think I've found the anaesthetist already," he said with a shot of remorse.

"Good. The others won't be far away. Get as much info on them as you can. And get those bloody papers back. That witch will have them still."

Myles desperately hoped that the witch would be wicked, conniving and dislikeable. Hopefully, though, she was colluding with these cunning rogues from the UK. They have it coming to them, he tried to convince himself. Unfortunately, the pool rescue episode sat uncomfortably amidst these thoughts. He thought of the Wizard of Oz, his favourite film as a child, but the newer plot of Wicked intervened. A transient mental image of himself as a Nazi collaborator, made him wince.

"Are you bloody listening to me?" came an insistent voice at the end of his phone. "You do know what is at stake here? The well-being of the innumerable patients throughout our United Kingdom."

Myles thought of the honours list.

"And you know what else it at stake…" The veiled threat hung in the air. Myles thought of his elderly parents.

"Yes sir," said Myles. "I'm well aware of exactly what is at stake here." There was a hesitation at the end of the phone. Followed by a small but perceptible lightening of tone.

"Well. Don't go getting yourself sunburnt. And put what you need on the bill," his boss added. "Though I'm not paying for anyone else."

Generous of you, thought Myles with irony. "Thank you," said Myles, with insincerity.

"Right. Well. Keep me informed Myles. Please." The call was terminated at the other end.

Myles was incredulous. His boss had addressed him by his first name and said "please" in the same sentence. Perhaps he was softening.

"Bloody poofter," the bowtie man in London said to himself as he hung up. "Hope he's not spending a fortune getting laid on my expense account." The world continued to rotate in its usual direction, thought God to himself. Or was it to herself?

*

Back in Manchester, a refreshed looking duo emerged from their room in the furthest reaches of the Manchester Lodge hotel, confirming that the mattresses really were as comfortable as claimed. Dave had slept soundly for the first time in months. Lexy had worn Sid's earplugs throughout the night, and Sid was too polite to tell them that they had both snored like drains in synchrony. They did go to the breakfast buffet, but sat at different tables initially as a precaution, hoping not to draw attention to themselves. As there were few others in there, they eventually joined each other in a far corner, away from the TV and trying to ignore the headlines. Sid had a vegetarian breakfast and Tom and Lexy opted for the carnivorous version, with an appropriate sense of combined guilt.

"Do you miss eating meat, Sid?" asked Lexy.

"I never have done. What you've never known, you don't miss." He smiled back gently.

"I hope you'd miss me," she said with a frown.

Sid looked back at her with a serious face. "Then I must never try meat. For, if it is anything like as addictive as you, I will immediately become an addict!"

Tom looked at Sid's endearing, transparent face. "Get a room, you two! And don't ever give charm lessons to Dave he said. Or even he'll get himself shagged to death within a week!"

Lexy scowled back. "Sid's a real gent," she said simply. "Anyway," she added "he knows to warn me if he's developing chest pains..."

They both hooted with laughter. Sid looked transiently mortified, but sensing their well-intentioned teasing, eventually smiled too.

"I hope no one is listening in to this conversation," he said. Fortunately, nobody was.

"Flights back this afternoon. Half four. Two seats together and then yours in the front," Tom said to Sid. Sid's face dropped.

"Sid I'm joking. Of course you're together. Could you both take a look through these papers in the meantime too, and see what you make of them? I'm hoping there's some additional thread in there between the RMC chief and these planned Government reforms, that I've missed."

"Perhaps they're on the same shift together at the soup kitchen for the homeless," suggested Lexy drily.

"I doubt it, but hopefully they'll soon be in the same soup," replied Tom with a grin. They finished their breakfasts, topped up their caffeine levels and got up to leave the breakfast area.

"We have a few hours left to kill," said Tom. "I'm going to pop back to the library. Do you want to join me?" They agreed to meet up there an hour or so later, after Lexy and Sid had tidied up a few loose ends of their own.

As they left, in the far corner, a TV headline declared 'private companies to take over NHS GP surgeries'.

"About bloody time," muttered the waitress. "I can never get to see my GP." All seventeen appointments in the last year had been a real struggle for her to get.

CHAPTER EIGHTEEN: FAX AND FIGURES

The right Honourable Damon Forester, Minister for Health, was on the telephone to one of his closest aides.

"Ray, this needs drip feeding in. Subtly. This morning's headline was a little premature…"

"My readers don't do subtle, Damon. They want drama. Change. And tits."

"Look, I'm not trying to tell you how to edit your paper," (he was) "but could you delay the next one for a couple of days at least?"

There was a pause at the end.

"Sir Ray has a nice ring to it," came the eventual reply, "don't you think?"

Damon hesitated. His allocation for the year had already been exceeded by rash promises.

"I'll do what I can. Just delay it. Soften it a little. Maybe dig around a bit more on our main protagonists."

"You mean further background checks?"

"Whatever you feel appropriate," replied the minister.

"Are we talking true, semi-true or complete fabrication, minister?"

"The usual level of complete truth only please," came the reply.

The editor grinned at the end of the phone. He recognised the code word giving the green light for him to print whatever he liked. The power of a regular political donation and a news company! He put the phone down and dialled a second number.

"Cheryl. Hi darling, how's things in the big city? I've got a little job for you. A mix of archaeology, history and fantasy required for your creative writing class. Need it back within the week. May be some sunshine in it for you too. You free?"

Cheryl checked her diary. A parents evening, anniversary meal and sports day. "Completely clear now," she replied. She pressed delete. She'd speak to the nanny later and she suspected her husband would have a better night without her anyway.

*

In the library, Tom had settled into a seat near the social justice section, where he suspected there would be the fewest people. He had spotted the same librarian from yesterday and noticed that she glanced in his direction intermittently. She looked vaguely familiar, but he'd seen so many faces over the years that he couldn't identify, who, when or where. She had a kind, pretty face, fair hair, and a slightly fuller figure than was Tom's usual 'type'. She was dressed in an understated fashion, with a simple white blouse, dark blue trousers, and flat shoes. After changing career to work in the library ten years or so previously, she could also now recognise those who regularly attended the library from those who were either in hiding, trying to keep warm or both.

She had recognised him immediately. Older face with fuller jowls than when younger, but still recognisable. She wondered why he had come to Manchester. He wasn't the type who usually frequented her library. She'd read the newspaper headlines, as all of the papers were kept in the current affairs section. She'd also noticed his sheaths of photocopying, and the subject matter the previous day.

Meanwhile, Tom sat quietly, searching through anything else he could find to link the RMC chief to a medical company or senior politician. There was so many medical articles that he wasn't sure where to start. He glanced at his watch. Half eleven.

Just as she was about to come over to talk to him, two others entered and walked towards him. The slim blonde woman was now talking to him, and Tom looked animated. She sat down again. Probably much more his type anyway, she thought. She shrugged and restarted her work, ordering new books and trying to decide which periodicals to cancel. When she looked up a few minutes later, they had all left. She rebuked herself for being stupid and continued her work. He probably wouldn't have remembered her anyway. Why would he?

*

In the home where smoke alarm detectors go to die, Ricky had read his mum's paper.

"Fack me!" he exclaimed. "I didn't realise it was this bad!"

"What's up with you?" asked his mother, who coughed loudly as she did so. A plume of cigarette smoke wafted from the kitchen table where she was sat.

"I think my bruv's in the deep doodlies," he replied. He lit a cigarette of his own and sat back, and as he did so, the parrot wolf-whistled from its cage next to the TV. "You're no bleedin 'elp!" he replied.

"Oi, that bird's been in the family twenty-five years!" said his mum.

"It's a miracle it's not got beak cancer by now," came the retort. "He's more addicted to bleedin tobacco than we are." Two simultaneous plumes of smoke entwined the trio.

The dog lay very still at floor level under the table. There was about six inches of breathable oxygen there still. He was the only mutt on the street with a smoker's cough. A quiz programme was on the TV. In between puffs on his cigarette, Ricky answered the questions correctly.

"I should be on the telly," he said. "I know more bleedin answers than they do."

"For £1,000, what do the initials MRI stand for in medicine?" asked the compere. "A) Marrow Replication Injections, B) Magnetic Resonance Imaging or C) Maintenance Renal Infusions?"

"I think I know this; I think it may be C," came the hesitant reply.

Ricky threw a fag end at the TV with a colourful torrent of expletives. "It's B, you stupid cow!"

"Would you like to use a lifeline?" asked the compere helpfully. A slight pleading note in his voice.

"She'll probably just hang herself with it," Ricky groaned.

"What's up with your friend then?" asked his mum. "Is it that one you used to drive around on the night shifts?"

Ricky grunted an acknowledgement. "Yep. Poor sod. Didn't realise it would blow up into this."

His mum laughed. "He weren't a bad doc neither. At least he went out, unlike some of the other lazy buggers. Wasn't he a bad tempered old git though?"

Ricky hesitated. "Not with me. He was alright. He knew I wouldn't take none of his shit anyway."

"Didn't he recommend you for that driving job at the

funeral directors too?"

Ricky winced. He'd rear-ended the funeral cortege in the second week. "Yep."

There was another pause. Having used her lifeline successfully, the contestant was now up to £2,000.

"Who wrote Wuthering Heights?"

"Ooh I know this, isn't it Charles Bronson?" came an excited squeal from the contestant.

Ricky couldn't bear it any longer. He turned the TV off in disgust.

"Oi I was watching that!" exclaimed his mum. Another wolf-whistle sounded from the corner. The dog held its nose closer to the floor in mounting desperation. Ricky took another look at the newspaper, and something stirred in his deep memory bank. His mouth opened and closed wordlessly. He stood up abruptly. "Mam, I've got to go out. Make a trip. Before it's too late."

"Where you going?" she asked. "You going to leave me on my own?"

"Tenerife."

"How long for?"

"Don't know. I'll bring you some cheap fags back, though," he promised.

She beamed and leant over to kiss him. "Good boy! When you going?"

"Now," he said.

"Bollocks," called the parrot. Followed by another wolf-whistle.

"You're not fackin cammin," came the instant reply. And with that, he tore a page out of the newspaper, picked up a small bag, took his passport out of the kitchen drawer and left the house. Ricky, that was. Not the parrot.

The dog let out a little whine.

CHAPTER NINETEEN: PRIVATISATION AND CONFIDENTIAL

By the time the plane landed in Tenerife, it was dark. Sid had slept for much of the flight, whilst Lexy had gone through the papers copied by Tom. She had underlined a few sections and put a circle around a couple of names, but nothing had really jumped out of the page at her.

It was clear that the private sector was being welcomed to bid for chunks of the NHS, which was nothing new in itself. A series of governments previously had already extolled the virtues of integrating the enormous historical capital investment made in the NHS by previous working generations with the ethics and long-term vision of the stock market. They relied on the gullibility of the average voter and the personality assassination of any dissenters, via the modern equivalent of the colosseum. The popular press. "Liars replacing the lions," as Tom said. "Power corrupts. Absolute power corrupts absolutely. Wise words of John Acton way back in 1887." History lessons since had clearly been missed.

In the meantime, the Crash Team were shortly due to reconvene in a local bar near the El Ole hotel. Rhiannon and Dave had spent a morning mainly in bed, followed by a walk along the coast, just holding hands. Words seemed superfluous. They'd met up with Ann and Diego later that morning, and Ann had expressed her combined surprise and delight with a single wink of her eye and a smile. Diego had slapped Dave on the back and kissed Rhiannon on both cheeks, with genuine warmth. He whispered something in Spanish to Ann and she responded by elbowing him in the ribs. Half nine and the seven of them were now sat together, sharing a jug of sangria and a few mixed plates of tapas, with a large lemonade for Sid.

It was dark, and nearby a different crooner sang 'My way'. The third outing for the song that evening, and this one with a Geordie twist. Frank Sinatra turned in his grave somewhere. Myles sat covertly nearby too. He had acquired a hat to disguise himself as a typical tourist. His pinkening skin was the better clue. One of Smiley's people, he was not. One of Pan's people, possibly.

Tom turned to the others. He smiled at Dave and Rhiannon in a paternal way. Dave gawped at Lexy's hair and Rhiannon nudged him before he could open his mouth.

"I'm changing it first thing in the morning," announced Lexy without anyone saying anything.

"Ok. An update. Sid, Lexy and I have sorted out our loose ends in the UK. The papers are having a field day at our expense. No surprise there."

"We saw," said Ann, although there was still some inherent delay in the British newspapers arriving there.

"It's also clear that the RMC have released information from our confidential files to them. The head has briefed them, and it looks like a witch-hunt will follow."

"Why us?" asked Dave.

"Wrong place, wrong time, that's all, I think," replied Tom. "Or perhaps right place, right time, for them. I think we represent the opening act. The distraction. The camouflage."

"Which is?"

"The long planned excuse to formally privatise large chunks of the NHS," said Tom. Sid nodded in agreement. "Starting with general practice."

"It's disgraceful. Surely the general public will object?"

"The general public voted this lot in," replied Tom. "They're getting what they want and deserve. It's just a pity for those who can't afford the alternative. Anyway, you can't vote if you're on a ventilator."

"A bit like car insurance premiums?" asked Ann.

"Not exactly," said Tom. "More like travel insurance premiums. No claims bonuses for the healthy and the reverse for the rest. Excess premiums for those with pre-existing disorders. Some, king-sized."

"A sort of bastard child of the NHS and private sector," said Sid. "Neither one thing nor the other."

There was silence. Everyone looked at Sid in shock. Myles, within earshot, shuffled uncomfortably in his seat.

"Bastard is not just a swear word," said Sid. "It can mean very difficult. Or lucky. But I use it in the sense of illegitimacy."

"So more like the American system?"

Tom nodded sadly. "Look at our senior politicians these days. Spot the similarity?"

Myles made a note, took an unwise gulp of his drink and a small ice cube decided to clamp his airway tightly shut. He tried to cough. Turned rapidly blue (masked by the dusk) and thrashed his limbs around. Hearing the commotion nearby the crash team leapt to their feet.

"He's having a heart attack!" screamed a nearby guest.

"He's choking!" echoed the medical trio, in unison.

Dave picked him up by the chest in a bear hug and pulled sharply. A small pebble of ice spectacularly launched itself across the bar hitting the bartender, a friend of Diego's, who ran over in alarm, thinking there was a fight starting. By now, Myles was at least breathing. He violently coughed a few times, and this was followed by a whimpering sound. Then he burst into tears.

As Lexy tried to comfort him, she noticed a small Dictaphone device on the floor next to him and a notepad. "He's a reporter!" she exclaimed. Then she recognised his face. "Oh my God. No he's not..."

Myles looked at her miserably. "No I'm not," he told the rest of them. He coughed again. "I'm worse than that."

"Not sure that's possible," responded Tom in surprise, who was extremely relieved that the man was now pink again. His lips matching his forehead. They sat him back in a chair as the barman came over to look at him. He was mainly relieved that it hadn't been a reaction to anything else in his drink.

"You ok, *amigo*?" he asked. Myles looked back into the concerned, deep brown eyes.

"*Sí*. Yes. I think so."

A moment passed as they gazed at each other.

"There's something in the bloody beer here," muttered Dave to himself, as he surveyed the scene. "We're in a bloody romcom!"

It took about ten more minutes for Myles to settle. Short bursts of coughing intervened at progressively longer intervals.

"Is there something you need to tell us?" asked Lexy. A guilt-ridden Myles nodded.

"Shall we get him some water?" asked Sid. "Perhaps without the ice this time?"

Dave smirked. "Is Sid suggesting we waterboard him?"

Rhiannon gave him a sharp kick. He yelped and shut up.

Lexy looked around to see if anyone else was showing interest in them. The drinkers at the bar had returned to the football, and a group of drunk British lads resumed their bar game of tossing peanuts at each other to catch in their open mouths.

"There truly is no hope for the planet!" said Tom in despair.

Sid turned to Myles. "Whoever you are, would you like to come back to our apartment where we can talk without being overheard? I promise you; you are perfectly safe with us. We are doctors," he added unnecessarily.

Myles looked at the seven friends. He thought about his boss, and his likely reaction. He looked over at the barman, who smiled back kindly. He knew that he had blown his cover, when Lexy had recognised him from The Wolf and Whistle excursions.

Ann reached out for his hand. "Come on," she said softly. "You look like you might need some after-sun too." She put the back of her hand on his forehead and tutted. "And Rhiannon has some milk chocolate."

Rhiannon frowned. Myles look into Ann's face. His mum used to stroke his forehead like that when he was a child. He got up and meekly followed her, and the rest followed him in a small procession. Rhiannon shot a glance at Dave, who was mouthing something to Tom and starting to do the conga. His grin froze and he carried on walking, obediently. Rhiannon turned back and couldn't resist a smile as she did. He was such a clown. But he was her clown. And he'd just saved another life.

Back in the apartment, Myles was looking a lot better. Ann had applied some after-sun to his nose and forehead. Rhiannon had broken off a generous chunk of her precious small supply of British chocolate, with a slight protest. The rest sat nearby but allowed him some space. They also left an open passageway to the exit, should he change his mind.

Even Tom expressed astonishment when Myles finally revealed whom he was working for. He tried to explain that his boss had threatened him if he didn't obey him, and Lexy correctly guessed the reason behind this, without voicing it.

Tom still looked astonished. "But why? Why us?"

"I don't think it's personal," responded Myles.

"It bloody feels it!" answered Tom. "What's in it for him?" Tom answered himself. "It is a bloody New Year's honours nomination, isn't it?"

Myles nodded miserably.

"And a promotion for you?"

Myles squirmed uncomfortably. "I think just not the sack. And not telling..." He stopped himself.

"Anyone about your personal life?" offered Lexy. She saw the alarm in his face. "Your family I guess. It's alright, your personal life should be just that."

"You must be feeling ashamed though." This came from Sid. "I don't mean about your personal life. I mean for potentially ending our careers. Our livelihoods. Our families. You are being a bastard to us." He looked incensed. The first time the others had seen him this way. Myles looked abjectly miserable.

Sid calmed a little and continued. "Perhaps you can help us though. Make it right. Regain your pride." Rhiannon shot Dave a warning glance before he said anything.

Myles looked back at them. "How?" he asked.

"Well, let's assume that you still send your boss information back about us, but this time we amend it a little. We... We embellish it a little."

Myles paused. "You mean, make me a double-agent?"

"Excellent idea, Moneypenny." Dave said to no one in particular. Rhiannon rolled her eyes in response. Myles clearly was warming to this latest idea.

"Your boss needn't find out either," added Sid.

And so a new plot was hatched. Myles, genuinely grateful that he hadn't choked to death on his first night in Tenerife, and also a little hopeful that perhaps the bartender might want to meet him again, agreed. He texted his boss *ALL WELL. SPOTTED THEM AND WILL REPORT BACK IN THE MORNING WITH NOTE.* Dave gave him a final brief medical check over and the group dispersed.

CHAPTER TWENTY: AS POPULAR AS...

Lancashire General Infirmary. 1988

"Good afternoon gentlemen and... lady. How are you all this fine day?"

The four students turned around from their hospital canteen seats to see a smiling, smart doctor in a crisp white coat. Tom looked uncertainly at the smiling face. He looked in his mid-twenties. He was at least two or three years beyond his house year days.

"I'm looking for two fit, strong medical students with an interest in advanced orthopaedic surgical techniques." The four faces continued to look back at him, wordlessly. His smile fell a fraction, but he continued to speak. "And it will be a fascinating morning in the latest theatre."

Still nothing.

"You get to wear a spacesuit..."

Tom's eyebrows raised involuntarily. There was a further pause.

"And there's a crate of Newky brown in it for the happy participants to share…"

"What would we have to do?" asked Tom.

"All you've got to do is hold a leg for the prof whilst he does a hip for an hour or so," replied the orthopaedic senior house officer with a benign grin.

Tom considered it. He was skint. He was interested in orthopaedics. He'd vaguely heard of the new air-fed spacesuits that the surgeons were trialling in the orthopaedic theatre to reduce the risk of post-operative metal joint infections. And he quite fancied the idea of a crate of Brown Ale too. He looked at his colleague, Andy.

"Why can't you do it?" asked Andy, who was the more streetwise of the two.

The SHO's face dropped. "I'm on a course. And I forgot to put a leave form in."

"And the prof will bollock you if you don't turn up in the morning…" Andy smiled now. A trace of malevolence visible. "I like Newky brown too," Andy said. "Sounds like thirsty work, that."

"Ok, two crates."

"And some crisps," added Andy. "Bacon ones. And prawn cocktail please." He was enjoying himself now.

"How about one of my bloody kidneys too?" said the SHO, who now looked like a typical, stressed junior doctor, akin to his colleagues. Andy considered answering in the affirmative, but decided he'd had his fun.

"Yep. Ok. Give us the details, but we need the beer first. We have a little pre-op party planned, don't we Tom!" Andy winked at the student to his left. "You free tonight, Kaz?"

Kaz beamed back.

Derek opened his mouth. "How about me too?"

"Nah, we don't fancy you, mate."

Tom shook his head. "Derek you'll be most welcome. Andy is a twat and will be in bed by ten at the latest."

"I certainly hope so," mouthed Andy in response.

*

The evening was somewhat of a blur. The bottled beer had an unusual, tangy taste.

"It's sort of more savoury than usual," said Tom. "I like it!"

"It's a tad out of date," replied Andy. "But if you try it with prawn cocktail flavour crisps it tasted even better. It'd make a nice stew." Andy put his hands in the large, opened bag, ate a large mouthful, and then smelled his fingers carefully. He paused for effect. "That reminds me, when's our gynae stint?"

Karen, the rather straight-laced but attractive Edinburgh student, slapped him playfully. "You're disgusting," she said.

"Go on, smell your hands, Tom, and tell me they don't…"

Tom smelt his own fingers. He spluttered on his crisps and a howl of laugher followed. This was followed by more brown ale. Soon the slightly more out of date crate, crate two, was being tapped.

"It's decent stuff this," said Tom. "Bet it'd make cracking gravy too!"

There were nods of approval. Derek was also nodding his head, but in the bathroom…

Finally, by about two in the morning, the motley crew decided to call it a night.

Tom belched loudly. "Oops!" There were giggles from the others.

Andy and Kaz waved and left unsteadily together, with their arms around each other. Andy grinned drunkenly back and gave a thumbs up.

"See you in the morning. Eight thirty sharp remember…"

"Oh shi… holy fuck," came the barely audible reply, but it was lost in the remnants of crisp packets and empty bottles. Tom somehow crawled to his bed and slept the sleep of the very drunk. His pillow fortunately absorbing most of his drool.

*

A hammering on his door awoke him. "Wake up, Major Tom, your spaceship awaits you!" came an insistent voice. "Planet earth is blue. And it's time for you to spew."

There was giggling from the two people on the other side. Tom sat up with a jolt and instantly regretted it. The room span like a waltzer. His stomach was gripped by a spasm and he just made it to the bathroom in time, as half of the contents of last night's beer session decanted with alarming speed but little precision, into the basin. He turned the taps on. Water threatened to overflow the small sink. He found a toothbrush and plunged it desperately around the sink's tiny opening. Little happened. A mixed essence of prawn cocktail and vomit steamed gracefully from the porcelain basin. Tom looked back at it in horror and tried to stifle the second wave of nausea. He didn't have time to go to the bathroom properly, and he looked longingly at the shower before shaking his head and throwing on some theatre blues from the end of his bed.

Thank God they won't be able to see me behind the face mask he thought. "Good morning professor, my name is Andy," he practiced. His contact lenses had clouded over as he'd fallen asleep in them. His eyes were red, and he couldn't see very well. He stepped out of his room. Karen looked at him with a genuine look of alarm on her face, but Andy lust laughed.

"Chundered yet?" he asked cheerfully Tom involuntarily wiped the corner of his mouth. The sink looked like a zombie had partially dissolved in it. "Goodo, you'll be fine now," he lied, then turned to Kaz and pulled a mock, horrified face, before turning back again.

"Tad late for brekkie alas," he added. "Mind you, there are few things less popular than a full honk in a spacesuit. Hi ho. Hi ho!" He whistled cheerfully and beckoned Tom to follow him.

When they arrived at theatre they were immediately scolded by the theatre sister. "Where the bloody hell have you two been?" she demanded.

"Late night feeding the homeless," replied Andy cheerfully. She looked at Tom's pale, unshaven face. "He's trying to look the part!" added Andy.

"Right, well, do exactly as the charge nurse says and leave your clothes in the changing room." The two looked startled. "You can keep your underwear on, stupid, but you need clean theatre wear inside those suits. And they get hot inside."

"What happens if you... if you need the toilet?" asked Tom.

"You'll need to go first. No chance once he's started the operation."

"And if you feel faint?"

"Just fall backwards, away from the surgical area please."

"And if we start floating around the room?" asked Andy innocently.

"Always a bloody comic amongst them," mumbled Sister to herself. "You've got five minutes, Abbott and Costello."

As they quickly got changed, Andy looked at his friend again. "What happened to your eyes?" he asked.

"Gas permeable lenses," replied Tom. "Not happy campers if you sleep in them. The room looks full of smoke now. It'll settle when I take them out, but I can't really see a bloody thing."

"Good job it's not brain surgery we're doing today then,"

smiled Andy. "They'd end up having a stroke. Not like the type Kaz gives though!" he smirked. "That Scottish posh totty likes a working-class man!"

Tom frowned. He liked Karen and had secretly hoped she might go out with him instead. Andy would ruin her.

"Right, step forward you two please." A pleasant student nurse helped each of them to get into the trouser section, to which was attached an air hose at the lower end. They both wriggled into them. Then the top half. They were both manipulated into the remainder of the suit, and a full head mask was then added.

"Are you feeling claustrophobic?" she asked.

"Not yet," replied Tom. "But I think I soon may be."

"You'll be fine. They're freshly filtered air fed. Fresh air in at one end, exhaust air out at the other."

Tom looked down. The mask obliterated what little remained of his central vision.

"Don't bend forward though," said the nurse. "You'll dislodge it."

Gloves followed and finally the two of them were ready for their first spacewalk.

"You look gorgeous, petal" said Andy. "Grey matches your skin colour."

"Fuck off I hate you!" replied Tom, ruefully. He repressed a simultaneous desire to belch and pass wind.

*

Around thirty minutes had passed. One of Tom's contact lenses had partially cleared but he still had little central vision in his right eye, which meant that he had to flick his eyes sideways to see anything.

"Will you keep your ruddy head still, doctor?" hissed the

professor. "Retractor," he demanded to no one in particular. With his helmet on, it was very difficult to work out to whom he addressed this particular command.

"Will you pass me the bloody retractor, doctor?" He now boomed with a muffled bellow. "And more swabs." (The wound was bleeding fairly actively still.) He was clearly becoming increasingly irritated. The heat, combined with the claustrophobia of the suit and the nature of the procedure. The incompetence of his assistant adding the crust to the crud pie of his day so far.

The hip was grotesquely positioned to enable the next part. Tom could read the words 'Black and Decker' on the drill. He gasped in surprise. This was of course, no ordinary household drill. Orthopaedic surgery was recognised as the finest form of joinery by those who undertook it as a medical speciality. Tom noted that those who practised this particular art were usually the rugby playing types who had drunk a lot of beer in their student days, shagged the most nurses and were adept at lifting heavy objects. What they lacked in brain they usually made up for in brawn. This pattern was to repeat.

The professor was an exception. He had never been able to hold his beer, was scrawny and hadn't had resits after failing the main summer exams. He was academic, awkward, and carried a plate of chips on each shoulder. He also disliked confined spaces.

Tom was sweating inside his helmet. The cold grey sweat that comes from drinking too much alcohol, not drinking enough fluid afterwards and discovering that the usually benign bacterial flora lining his bowel had undergone a brisk and hostile takeover. His abdominal colic was increasing to danger levels. Tom undertook a risk assessment whilst trying to hold the patient's leg still. Air fed into the top of his helmet he reasoned, and out of the bottom. If he had to pass wind, it should bypass his head completely. He waited for a lull in the surgery, and he relaxed his sphincter. Mercifully, the hiss of escaping gas was inaudible to all. For a full three seconds, Tom felt the relief.

The next moment, it was as if a cloud of noxious swamp gas, combined with a swarm of wasps, had simultaneously invaded his helmet. He visibly gasped.

"You need to keep still," said the nurse by his side. Fortunately, the professor hadn't noticed yet. Tom nodded and held his breath.

Finally he decided to breathe through his mouth in case he fainted. A minute passed. He chanced a tenuous breath through his nose. Risk of spontaneous explosion status had reduced to a mere 'possible gas leak'. He sighed with relief. Andy just about visible on his opposite side, was now shaking intermittently. Tom wondered generously if this was from a similar affliction, but Andy was simply trying to stifle his convulsions of laughter, camouflaged by his futuristic fancy dress outfit.

Another thirty minutes passed. By now, Tom had managed to time the airflow rate through his suit fairly accurately. He would hyperventilate until his lips just started to go numb, expel another salvo of flammable gas and then hold his breath to the count of thirty. It was unpleasant still, but at least he now felt he had similar odds of surviving the operation as the patient.

Finally, and to Tom and Tom's olfactory system's enormous relief, the ordeal was over. The professor, relieved to imminently be released from his confinement, thanked the staff, and exited the theatre stage left.

"You alright, laddie?" asked the anaesthetist kindly, who had quietly observed the whole drama.

Tom nodded. "Will be soon."

And that was it. Tom walked gingerly towards the changing room. Andy followed with a grin. Tom looked at him menacingly. "Not a word. Not one fucking word."

And for once, Andy's brain managed to override his mouth. With that, Tom headed slowly but purposefully towards sanctuary. The changing room and in particular, the gents toilet. Meanwhile, the auxiliary nurse, who had been sat outside the enclosed operating tent area next to the air outlet exhaust, was phoning her manager about an unpleasant gas leak she thought she had smelt throughout most of the operation. After a temporary closure for safety checks, the orthopaedic theatre reopened the following week.

*

In fact, two aircraft had touched down within a short time of each other at Tenerife South airport. The first contained a cabin full of cheerful Mancunians with some additional Scousers, who had collectively emptied most of the duty-free stock on board. A second containing a more sober group from the South East of England. Amongst these was a sharp featured, perma-tanned, middle-aged woman. She had hand luggage only, wore a sharp business suit and clutched a phone which she had stealthily attempted to use throughout the flight. The female of the spider species. Beautiful but with a deadly web and a poisonous kiss. She liked to research her victims as much as she could. Learn their habits and weaknesses. Understand their habitat. She was an assassin. Of characters.

The remit she had been given by her old boss had been brief but specific. "Dig some dirt, Cheryl. Big boss says we may need it, in case we need a bargaining chip or two. They're rotten apples to the core. And if they're not, improvise. Spoil 'em! And I don't mean with treats."

"They'll be hooch when I've finished with them," she had replied with a sneer.

The anaesthetist's story had been the most juicy. Whilst

builders deal with snagging lists, Dave's projects, it seemed, swapped the 'n' for an 'h'. She knew how to deal with him. Predictable, testosterone-laden chauvinist. Sid had a weakness for dominant women and was easily bullied. She let out a sharp laugh. He would soon be toast then. Tom? Alcohol! She smiled and patted the duty-free purchase reassuringly at her side. It also contained a bottle of Chanel for her favourite person.

Before the plane had even stopped, she had her seatbelt off and was ready to leave the aircraft, at speed. She was sat at the very rear and knew that this was the quickest place to exit. She had slid through passport control despite a slight delay, ignored the offers of free maps and went straight out of the airport, past the taxi rank and straight towards the bus stop. She reached into her bag, drew out a lighter and lit a cigarette. She inhaled deeply. How she hated flying.

"Got a light *Señorita*?" She turned around in surprise. "Don't suppose you've got a fag I can have too have you?"

She looked into the eyes of a stocky, unshaved man with piercing blue eyes and a mischievous grin. The corner of her mouth and a single eyebrow twitched involuntarily. He was around five foot eight inches tall and wore an old black t-shirt with the legend 'Black Sabbath' emblazoned, and aged black jeans. "Do I know you?"

He smiled back. "Don't fink so darlin'. Not unless you work for probation?" She recoiled slightly. He laughed. "Joking! Honest. I don't bite! Unless you're a rare steak."

"It looks like you've got a lifetime supply of your own cigarettes down there," she said and with a withering stare, pointed at his carrier bag.

"Yeah, but they're shit ones for me and me mam when I get 'ome. Yours smell like decent ones."

She paused. "Will you promise never to speak to me again if I do?"

186

Ricky looked genuinely hurt. Fackin 'ell, who pissed on your chips, he thought to himself? "Only if you promise to marry me immediately."

There was another pause. And then, unguarded for a moment, she laughed. Briefly albeit, then recovering her light sneer. "You can have one then, but you really wouldn't want to marry me. I'd eat you for breakfast."

"Promises!" he said quietly. He looked lovingly at the cigarette she'd given him. "I'll treasure it forever!"

"You don't want a light then?"

"Well if you must," he replied. "Sorry mate," he addressed the cigarette. "It's all in a good cause."

She lit his cigarette and he smelt a fresh waft of Chanel as she leant towards him.

"Fack, you smell better than the fags."

"I must tell Chanel, they'll be overwhelmed. Tell me, do you work for a charm school?"

"Royals only," responded Ricky in between billows of blue smoke.

"That fits," she replied.

He paused. "Ricky," he said and proffered a slightly grubby outstretched hand.

"Martha," lied Cheryl. Though to her surprise, she offered hers too.

He kissed her hand gallantly. "Well, Maybe catch ya in the resort later for a sangria, Martha," he added with a grin. "This your bus?" A bus pulled over.

He had distinctly heard the passport officer call her Cheryl, Mrs Cheryl Markides, as she'd gone through the control point and he'd double checked her photo. An unusual name. Greek? Still, she smoked decent fags and had a decent figure too. And he quite liked sangria.

He got on. She didn't.

Chapter Twenty-One: Cockney Slang

Sid, who had seemed very unsettled the night before, was now laid quietly next to Lexy in their room. He was thinking. Sid wondered how his son was managing back home. As much as he tried, he couldn't help worrying about his wife too. Where would she be now? (As it turned out, she was on her way towards a phone signal in Luxembourg.) Lexy turned towards him and held his hand. She could sense his unease.

"What's up?" she asked gently. "Can I help?"

Sid was silent for a few moments. "I always just feel so guilty," he replied.

"About what?" She stroked his hair softly.

"About everything really."

"You're Indian," she replied. "Guilt is inbuilt. It's who you are."

He turned to look at her and smiled. "Why so wise?" he

asked. He kissed her forehead. She kissed him back.

"Because I've seen everything."

Soon the two were sensuously entwined under the sheets.

"Do you love me?" she asked.

"Without hesitation," he replied. "Do you love me?"

She hesitated. For effect. And then kissed him fully on the mouth. "God only knows why but yes!"

A mix of exhilaration and terror ran through Sid's body. He was in uncharted seas now. He felt eighteen again.

*

Back in London, events had been unfolding rapidly. Keen to receive his updates from Myles, the bowtied man was now pacing up and down the floor of his opulent office. He was on his phone.

"Yes. Yes… of course… Don't be an arse, of course he will… I'm aware of that. I'm sorry…" And then a long pause as he listened to the voice on the other end of his phone. "Well, she bloody well better had. And quickly!" The conversation was terminated, and he reached for the decanter on the walnut desk, pouring himself a long drink. He didn't like the newspaper proprietor, but he knew the maxim… and he kept his enemies closer still. The minister for health had asked to speak to him later over lunch. He was aware that it hadn't been a request, it had been an order. In the meantime, he still hadn't been able to locate the files, within which he knew that his fate lay. He opened his newspaper.

'Your life in their hands' the title had read. A comprehensive but extremely selective post-mortem followed, regarding the careers of a small cross-section of the medical fraternity who had erred. Top of the list was Dave the Anaesthetist.

'He took advantage of me in the recovery room' screamed the first title. Followed by a series of fairly revealing photos of the advantaged recovery nurse.

'He cremated our crematorium' read the next, illustrated by a litre bottle of Jack Daniel's and a very young photograph of Tom at a party as a junior doctor.

The only photo of Sid had been from his class graduation ceremony, and they had labelled the wrong person. "They all look the bloody same, it won't matter who," came the advice from the newspaper editor. 'The perils of self-prescribing…' Followed by a fairly graphic account of Sid's subsequent confidential medical consultation with his GP.

Finally, another very old photograph of Lexy astride a motorcycle but wearing full leathers this time. At least this one was a flattering image. She looked like she just had walked off a Meatloaf music video. It had been skilfully photoshopped. 'Biker siren seduces runaway docs!' ran the headline.

An editorial followed, in which a balanced and neutral overview was not offered, ending with a recommendation that 'your life is not safe in their hands' and that carefully selected health provision by the private sector might offer the only salvation, following 'years of abuse by the doctors working within the NHS'. Comment offered by an unnamed source from the department of health was quoted as saying, 'We will do everything we can to protect the safety of the general public and to continue to strive to provide the best health care in the world for all. Every option will now need to be carefully considered'.

Meanwhile in the finance section, the share price of half a dozen companies gained measurably.

*

Cheryl had quietly checked into her five-star hotel the night before, fairly close to the waterfront. 'Adults only' it promised. The pool area was the epitome of peace and sterility. She had purposefully settled for a sunbed in part shade, the least overlooked but with a good view of the surrounding poolside area. A half-filled ashtray lay to her right side, with a vodka and tonic next to that.

To her other side lay her sleek smartphone. Well used and permanently connected to the hotel's internet. She was clearly leafing through a number of articles. Pressing the screen 'save' button intermittently. She gestured to a waiter in immaculate white, and another ashtray and a fresh drink were brought.

*

In a nearby apartment block with five fewer stars, Ricky looked at his swimming trunks. Last worn at least two decades earlier, with little chance of retaining dignity, never mind anything else. Ricky looked across at the luxurious gated hotel in the distance. He had a pretty good idea that this was the only hotel which she would find sufficient for her demanding needs, and he determined then and there to explore the place as soon as possible.

At the pool bar, 'two pints - one euro' beckoned, but Ricky didn't drink.

"Fancy a beer mate?" asked the owner. More Cockney than Canarian.

"Nah, mate, I'd rather have something soft," replied Ricky. And he sat at the empty bar on the least broken barstool. He looked around. The pool had once been a place of tranquillity. The water still looked blue and reasonably inviting, but the paving stones which made up the floor, were grubby and cracked. The bottom edges of the pool looked less inviting. Ricky could see that one of the pumps was blocked, and a variety of uninspiring looking objects, had sunk into the abyss here and there. Some animate at some time and some not. The small number of white plastic sun loungers were, without exception, all broken in at least one place. Most of the ashtrays spilt over with cigarette ends.

"How long have you had this place?" asked Ricky.

The scrawny tattooed barman flipped the end of his cigarette into the beleaguered shrub behind him and gave Ricky a sideways glance before replying.

"Too long. Used to run it with the missus but she went off with a local karaoke singer a few years ago. My bleedin' Way. It's a shit heap now but I just can't be bothered and there's nothing for me back home. At least the fags are cheap out here." He drew himself a pint of lager in a plastic cup, having first removed another stray cigarette end from it.

"It has…" Ricky's voice hung in the air briefly, "potential!" he finally said. "It's not even far from that posh place over there." He pointed at Cheryl's likely hotel.

"One hundred and twenty euros a night without even a bleedin' sea view!" exclaimed the barman in disgust. "We charge twenty!"

Ricky stifled a reply.

"Have you ever been inside?" he finally asked.

"Yeah, but that was a long time ago in the scrubs."

"Nah, mate. I mean the hotel over there." He pointed.

"Ah, yeah. Now and then. They sell the same bleedin beer I do here for five times the price, you know! Daylight robbery's what I say."

"Yeah, but can you go in there for just a drink?"

"Don't tell me you're about to have a beer over there now!?"

Ricky calmed him. "No I'm just… trying to meet up wiv someone in there. A lady."

The barman's face lit up. "You could bring her over here. It's half price cocktails later, six 'til seven."

Ricky grimaced. "I could certainly ask her. Is there a tradesman's entrance?"

The barman grinned back. He handed him a full crate of beer. "You go round the kitchen and say Des sent you. They'll let you in. Cost you twenty euros for the beer though."

Ricky looked back. "Ten," he said. They agreed on fifteen.

"Er, you might want this too." He gave Ricky a once white barman's apron. "Disguise," he added, helpfully. "'Ope she's worth it" he added. "Watch out for the bloody crooners!"

"So do I," said Ricky. "You ain't got a pack of cards I could borrow 'ave you, bruv?"

*

Tom, Dave, Lexy and Sid had all agreed to meet up again in the small local café, close to where Diego lived. Tom was developing a tan and had lost some more of his alcohol-induced midriff. Dave looked relaxed and Sid seemed similarly calm. All were dressed in casual clothes which were better suited to the surroundings than their original ones.

"Do you trust him?" asked Dave eventually.

"Wiley Myley? I'm not sure yet," replied Tom. "He looks pretty genuinely scared of his boss though, and I can't see Sid competing with that."

Lexy turned around. "I do," she said. "I've seen him with his creepy boss many a time back at my old pub. He's a coward but basically he's not bad. Believe me, I can tell!"

"So what's the plan?" asked Tom simply. "Do we let him into our little fold or not?"

"I suggest partially," said Lexy. "Test him out a bit first. Feed him some titbits and see where they end up."

"Don't think he's into tits!" grinned Dave. Everyone ignored him.

"You mean we write his script for him?" questioned Sid.

"Yes. Ground bait again."

"Have you ever actually been fishing?" asked Tom. They all looked at Dave, awaiting more profundity.

"Well actually, I used to go a lot. Ground bait can confuse fish. They end up eating it all and then don't have any appetite left for what's presented on the main hook." To their joint surprise, they had to acknowledge that Dave had a point.

"So what do you suggest, Captain Ahab?" asked Tom.

Dave looked blank. "From 'Moby Dick'." said Lexy.

"Ok, Captain Birdseye then?"

"Ah! Well I just think that time isn't on our side, and if we need to do something, we probably need to do it fairly quickly."

"Like?"

"Like finding out if old bowtie himself has a vested interest in one of these companies who stand to gain by general practice being upended and privatised."

"And then?"

"Well, I hadn't really got any further than that."

Lexy looked in deep concentration. She was trying to remember something. A small fact, buried somewhere in her memory.

"I do remember him talking to Myles about some shares he'd bought. He was bragging as usual, and said they were going to go bananas within the next year. It was some small medical tech company. He said they didn't know it yet, but that they were going to be chosen for the next wave. He just didn't say what the next wave was about or what a wave is."

Dave gave a little wave. They laughed.

"Can you remember what the company was called?" asked Tom.

"No I can't, but I do remember that he told Myles that he'd need to buy some for him."

"But that's insider trading!" remarked Sid. "It's illegal!"

"And immoral," replied Tom. "Perhaps a little added bonus in case the knighthood didn't come off?"

"Time for a little chat with Myles," said Lexy." Perhaps we should head over to last night's bar again…" She smiled knowingly to herself.

*

At Luxembourg airport, a harassed looking lady hailed a taxi to take her to a hotel nearby. "Bastard!" she hissed to herself. "I've got him now!"

CHAPTER TWENTY-TWO: UNPROTECTIVE SUNSCREEN

"Mam. Mam it's me. Ricky!"

"Are you alright?" A cacophony of coughing followed. A coughophony.

"Well you're still bleedin breavin', at least! Mam, I'm going to be here a bit longer. You got enough grub in?"

"Bollocks," came the shrill reply.

"Well, I'm glad he's still alive too."

Eventually, they managed to have a brief conversation. the gist of which was that he had to remain in Tenerife for another couple of weeks, and that Sooty had enough bird food to be able to continue issuing expletives until Ricky came back, whilst Sweep also had enough dog food, if his doggy lungs held out that long.

He pressed the 'end call' button. He did worry about her. Even cared for the bloody parrot and the mutt. They didn't really have anyone else.

"Bollocks," he said to himself and smiled. He picked up

the beer crate and turned towards the hotel.

*

The crate of beer had worked like a charm. Des was clearly well liked in this part of the town. It turned out he had once been a half decent karaoke singer in his own right, and had even been a regular singer at the hotel itself a few years previously. Ricky managed to cadge a couple of Spanish cigarettes from one of the waiters, and then walked across to the outside bar. The apron hadn't been needed, and so he rolled it up and put it back in his pocket, creating an unsightly bulge.

He smelt her before he could see her. A waft of Silk Cut and Chanel No5. A smoking concoction anywhere. He decided to stay just out of her direct line of visibility so that he could watch her without being seen himself. She was on her phone and seemed to be having a fairly animated conversation with whoever it was on the other end. It didn't take him long to confirm that Martha/Cheryl had not come to Tenerife to sample the sunshine and vodka tonics. He heard her saying that she was "going to take a closer look later that evening", but he couldn't hear anything else. Whoever was at the other end was in no doubt that she was calling the shots. She terminated the call and lit another cigarette. He could see her scowl.

She then made another call, but this was made in more hushed tones, and at the end of this one, he saw her wipe an angry tear from one of her eyes. A mouthed expletive had followed.

His original plan had been to try to find her, cadge a cigarette or two off her, generally charm her and then attempt to get any information out of her that he could. Plan B now beckoned. He decided to remain undercover. A waiter approached him and offered him a towel robe. "Sir, a drink?

Maybe one of your beers?" he winked at Ricky.

"Not quite yet. Fanks, though. Perhaps just a glass of water. Not bottled though."

He went over to a vacant lounger and put the pristine white item on. The effect was transforming. Soon, a glass filled with icy water ice and fruit arrived. Ricky smiled to himself. "Bladdy ell, I could do this for a livin'."

Martha, or should I say Cheryl, was tapping on her phone. She seemed to be taking notes, and then transferring these to a different file on her tablet device. He was glad he had shaved before leaving his own apartment a spare razor left by the room's last incumbent in the bathroom. The effects had been transforming on his appearance, though he was developing a slight rash. Ricky naturally had some skin colour, given that his own father had been Cypriot. The snake tattoo along his forearm was covered by the robe. He'd even picked up a discarded Spanish magazine to complete the look, through which he'd cut a number of small peep holes. The effect was probably more Carry On than Le Carré, but Cheryl was so engrossed in her own actions that she seemed unlikely to notice him across in the far corner.

He laid there for a while. He had to admit, his planning hadn't really extended this far. He was already feeling pretty pleased with himself for getting successfully to Tenerife in one piece, and then managing to find Cheryl in the resort. It was the only five-star hotel there, but still, he felt pretty smug. In fact, he hadn't really had any plan at all, just a basic desire to help his friend, however he could. He decided that his next step was to try to intercept the phone calls she was making. Ricky was not particularly successful in his day job, from which he had recently been dismissed after threatening to demonstrate how his boss's pen could be used as a proctoscope, but he did have an encyclopaedic knowledge of minor facts, and a photographic memory. He also had an IQ somewhere above one hundred and fifty. A fact that was very well hidden from the naked eye.

The name Markides did ring a bell, somewhere in his brain. He was pretty sure it was a Greek name. He would have taken a look on the internet, had his phone been any good. His was the type that was only any good for phoning people and retaining a battery life for more than an hour. He was rather painfully aware that his 'bruv', Tom, had no idea that he was trying to find him. His cash supplies were also perilously low.

Ricky's relationship with Tom had been an interesting one. They had first met when Tom was a GP, working on the out-of-hours circuit, and Ricky had been his driver technician. The two had got along instantly, and quickly developed a brotherly bond, despite the apparent chasm in their own backgrounds. Ricky had a strong moral compass and ethical code, which he compromised for neither man nor beast. It had got him into a lot of trouble in the past, particularly with employers, but his refreshing honesty had also won him loyal plaudits. He had quickly recognised Tom's weaknesses, particularly for alcohol, and had covered up on a number of occasions when Tom really shouldn't have been at work at all.

He had admonished Tom on one particular occasion. "Do that again, and you're fackin toast, mate. You're not treating my bleedin parrot in that state."

It had had the desired effect. One of the first wake-up calls that Tom had needed. Issued with just the right balance of menace and concern. He turned up sober for every shift after then. Their friendship had developed over the years they worked together, with each recognising some of their own failings in the other. Since Tom had been suspended, they hadn't had much contact. It was a pity, as whatever Tom lacked in the emotional stability department, he compensated for in clinical acumen and a desire to do the right thing. He was an astute clinician, with a sixth sense of whenever a patient needed urgent action. They made a good team.

Cheryl ordered and quickly emptied her third glass of vodka tonic. Then she got up, walked a little unsteadily towards the far doors, leaving her phone alone on the table. Ricky wasn't quite sure what he was going to do, but he decided to nonchalantly walk past the table, pick up her phone, and then adlib from there. There were so few other people in the pool area, it didn't take him long to arrive at her table, pick up her phone and go back to his own lounger. He just hoped she hasn't set her phone to facial recognition or some bloody awful password.

It was locked. Please enter passcode, it requested. Ricky tried to think fast. People tend to use their date of birth for a six-digit code. Something memorable? Clearly, that would also be pretty easy to open if you knew the person. The only problem was that he didn't know her date of birth. He also doubted that it would work. But as he'd watched her on her phone, he'd noticed that she seemed to use a figure trace pattern on the screen rather than enter digits each time she picked it back up.

He looked at the phone screen by tilting it towards the light. Thank goodness for sun-cream. He could just make out what appeared to be a continuous recent smear in between the multiple dots, and when he tried this, the phone magically sprang into life. He looked anxiously across towards the door. She still hadn't returned. He knew that he didn't have very much time, and so he jotted down the last two numbers in the phone call history into his magazine. Presumably, her boss followed by her husband or lover. He did a quick search on her internet history and jotted that down too.

Then, he entered the first number into the phone's screen, and the initials CB came up. He blocked the contact's phone number then replaced it with his own in the phone's memory for CB. He couldn't think of anything else, and he realised that he didn't really have any more time anyway. With that, he locked the phone again walked back over to her bed and replaced it on the table. Just as he did so, he saw her emerge from the other side of the hotel.

Desperately hoping she hadn't seen him, he continued walking casually towards the other end of the pool, stood under the icy shower, cursing quietly to himself as he did so, and then got into the pool. A few more people had come down to the pool area over the past few minutes, and so he hoped that she hadn't noticed him. He also felt fairly sure that the pool was the last place she'd be coming to, given her expensive haircut and recently re-applied suntan oil.

There was only one minor problem. Ricky couldn't swim. He was terrified of water, and just hoped that he had got in at the shallow end. Fortunately, he had and so he simply sat there. Water up to his waist. Trying to look relaxed.

After fifteen very cold minutes, during which he still managed to perspire continuously from his forehead, he clambered slightly awkwardly out of the opposite poolside end. Slipping slightly on the stepladder on the way out. He deliberately avoided looking over at Cheryl's sunbed. Hopefully, she wouldn't have noticed that her phone had changed position slightly on the table…Or been cleaned…Or even the hole in his shorts.

*

Across at the El Ole, Tom was lying on his front. Thinking. For the first time in more than two weeks, he missed a drink. An unnatural craving threatened to overtake him. He could feel a cold sweat breaking out all over his body. He was trying to work out what he was going to do with the rest of his life. Dave was smitten with Rhiannon, and Sid and Lexy were similarly inseparable. What was wrong with him, he wondered?

He'd loved his first wife yet really hadn't given her any choice but to leave. Even he admitted that he'd been unbearable. Stubborn. Single minded. Addicted. It made for a good script but an unhappy ending. It went around and around in his head, making it hurt. He tried to think about when it had all started to really unravel. He remembered all too painfully missing the abnormal heart tracing on the child. The awful aftermath. And having to intubate the stabbing victim whilst still awake. He could still see the face staring back at him. His mistakes haunted him, but things had eventually seemed to fall into a sort of perspective.

And then he realised. It was losing an enormous, extended family of two and a half thousand, one by one. Some in road accidents. Others by suicide or with cancer or acute illnesses. Some quickly and some agonisingly slowly. He recalled the feeling of panic and impotency. Of not being able to do anything, multiplied and repeated over the following years.

It was a huge, fathomless loss. People he had known for years and really cared about. He couldn't even bear to keep the thank you cards anymore from their relatives. His head hurt, and now, he could feel the tears come, and they just kept coming in a steady, constant stream. He tried to think of as many of the names and faces as he could. Perhaps that would at least give him some sort of closure. The young, the old. The frightened.

He often marvelled at how just a few simple words of heartfelt kindness given at the right time could make such a difference. When in reality, he was floundering as to what to do next. And then he decided what he needed to do now. He tried to wait until his eyes were less red and he could breathe through his nose again, this took quite a few minutes. Then he quietly got up and put his long-sleeved shirt on.

"Need some company?" asked Sid gently.

What was it about Sid? He seemed to be able to see deep into his very soul. He hesitated. "That's really kind Sid, but I think I need to do this myself."

Sid placed a hand on his shoulder and smiled. "Don't do anything silly. I'd never forgive myself. Promise…"

Tom managed a small smile back, said, "Promise," and walked steadily away towards the pool exit.

"Will he be ok?" asked Lexy.

"I think he needs to exorcise some demons," said Sid.

Dave, who was half listening, mumbled something about exercise being a very good thing for the mind and soul, and carried on reading his paper about a celebrity with a large bottom.

"You are Palaeolithic man personified," said Lexy. Sid nodded in agreement.

"Is that good?" asked Dave.

"Your pet woolly mammoth would think so!" she retorted.

*

In a quiet corner of the old church, Tom sat very still, with his head bowed. He'd lit a few candles and was now muttering something to himself and no one else in particular. It seemed like a series of names. Whatever it was that he was saying, he could feel the weight of the world lifting gradually from his shoulders. And as it did, the desire to have a drink simply disappeared too. An hour or so must have passed. He'd fallen asleep, slumped forward into the pew in front of him.

A kindly voice eventually stirred him. "*¿Estás bien, hijo mío?*"

Tom looked at the kindly, creased face. "*Sí. Padre. Soy ahora. Gracias. Lo Siento.*"

"*No necesitas decir lo siento,*" came the reply. The priest touched his head and made the sign of the cross.

"Te perdonan. Ir y vivir su vida."

And with that, Tom simply stood up, emptied his pocket of coins into the small collection box near the door, looked back across to the altar one last time and left through the side door. He felt the sun beating down on his face. And paused for a moment. It felt so good.

CHAPTER TWENTY-THREE: THE LIBRARIAN

A long way away, in a Mancunian library, the librarian had been pouring through a series of articles in the archives. As usual during the early Autumnal months, the library remained reasonably quiet. Students weren't yet panicking about their Christmas exams, and the weather wasn't cold enough to bring in many of the heat-seekers from the streets.

She'd been following the newspaper headlines over the past few days and was aware of the political storm-clouds that were developing, particularly over the NHS. The opposition parties had been in disarray over the past few years, and a series of infighting episodes, inflated massively by the popular press, had effectively negated their ability to pass much in the way of an authoritative opinion on the important issues of the day. Their credibility had been systematically undermined to such a degree that they no longer seemed to hold any real, effective role any more. Look at the Americans. They'd just appointed a narcissistic, racist clown as president by popular vote. Stupidity seemed to offer no barrier to power these days.

She'd accumulated three piles of documents. The first of these she labelled 'A' and put a green clip across. The second pile 'B' she clipped together with a yellow one, and the third 'C' with the red clip. Suzanna, Suzie to her friends, then tried to decide what to do with the information she had gathered. She'd made fairly copious notes across most of the documents, with a series of cross-references. She then attached the cuttings that she had taken from the recent newspapers and put these all into a large plastic wallet.

Well that was the easy bit. What was her intention now? Although she'd managed to acquire a significant amount of evidence, she didn't really know what to do with it next. She went into her work account on the computer and checked her annual leave entitlement. Unsurprisingly, she still had at least four weeks left to take until the end of the financial year, and this didn't include the previously untaken leave from the year before.

It wasn't that Suzie didn't enjoy holidays, it's just that there wasn't really anywhere she wanted to go by herself. She liked feeling the warmth of the sun on her body, enjoyed painting the waves on her canvases and ached for genuine and lasting romance. As a student nurse all those years ago, she had been to all the parties, met all of the pseudo-charming men at them and been emotionally abused in the process. She'd been promised the world, only to discover that the world wasn't theirs to give. A deep desire to have children had never been fulfilled and following one particularly unhappy romantic entanglement with a married consultant, she'd left the profession altogether to take up her second great passion; books and reading. On the positive side, this gave her lots of time to read, and a first-hand opportunity to discover some of the truly great masterpieces which had been created over time.

Whilst she did love the world's recognised classics, she also found a real thrill in stumbling across an undiscovered author who had managed to expose their very soul within the safety of a book's cover. She'd always intended to write her own story but didn't really feel that anyone would be interested enough in hearing it. It had been a relatively uneventful life. Heartbreak is widespread out there and she had not acquired any particularly interesting diseases.

The life and loves of a Mancunian librarian didn't seem the most likely best-seller title for a book. Maybe a Booker prize though?

She looked at the newspaper again. Tenerife. She recognised the resort too. Was her passport still in date, she wondered? And what would she wear anyway? Then she remembered something that might still be a perfect fit.

*

"Bruv! Bruv it's me, Ricky!"

Tom squinted at his phone again. He'd been asleep for at least an hour on the stone steps and was slightly disorientated still when he'd answered it.

"Ricky, where are you?" he asked. He felt like his brain has just undergone a factory reset.

"Um… did you manage to sort the car and those cards out? Has something gone wrong?"

"Of course. And of course not, in that order. Fink I'm some sort of amateur?" came the response. "All sorted and I am sat across the square, looking at you. I think you may have sunstroke."

Tom laughed. "Hilarious! How is Doncaster?"

"Wouldn't know," came the reply. "But that woman in

orange trousers on your left didn't half just give you a dirty look!"

Tom immediately awoke. He stood up and looked across the cobbled square.

"Well bugger me…" was the only reply he could offer; his mouth fell open in surprise. Ricky bounded over to him and gave him an enormous hug.

"Gotcha!" he said with a huge beam.

"Your mum?" asked Tom suddenly in alarm.

"Still alive," replied Ricky. "Daft old cow. She's gotta stay alive to feed the dog. And the parrot."

An unpleasant transient image crossed Tom's mind if the dog's food ran out and he sought revenge against his mistress…

"I'm… I'm overwhelmed. How did you get here?"

"By jet ski and open swimming mainly," replied Ricky. "How the fack do you think I got here?! Anyways, I have some important information for you, and I need your help with the next bit. Can we go to your Batcave please?"

Tom smiled. He was genuinely both delighted and overcome to see his friend. To his recollection, Ricky hadn't gone further south than Battersea in his entire life. He hugged him again. "You crazy cockney bastard!" he said with genuine affection.

"Right. Well. To the Batcave it is… By the way, where are you staying?"

"At a lesser known branch of the Hilton," replied Ricky. "You must come see it, old chap." He grinned. A childlike but genuine beam of delight.

CHAPTER TWENTY-FOUR: THE BATCAVE

The Crash Team welcomed its latest new member at the poolside. Ricky was quick to crack some witty retorts, and very soon he looked like he'd always belonged there with them. Dressed casually now in a light blue shirt (one of Tom's) and having replaced the heavy jeans with a pair of baggy shorts, he looked and felt more relaxed. Sid was initially a little cautious, as he spotted Ricky raise his eyebrows at Lexy walked towards them, but he soon relaxed.

"Well bruv," he said finally. "What have you lot been up to, eh?! Is Lord bleedin Lucan round here too?"

They laughed and Tom briefly updated him of events so far. Fortunately, their end of the pool was relatively private. Ricky looked stunned.

"So a nice, quiet jolly for you lot then!" He finally added with irony.

"Well, I think I've made a connection of my own. Though I'll need your help." He showed them his phone message from Cheryl. 'Silky Lady' it came up in his phone.

Ricky grinned. "After the brand of her favourite fags." He shrugged his shoulders.

"Romance isn't dead, eh?" replied Tom. He read the message.

ON TO THEM. HOW LONG DO YOU NEED? C X

He forwarded it to another number in his phone, under the name Ed.

WTFRU? came the reply a few moments later. Then another. *NEEDED PRONTO! DEADLINE 6PM TOMORROW YOUR TIME. DON'T LET ME DOWN.*

Tom looked baffled.

"Long story bruv," said Ricky. "I've borrowed a contact number from a reporter from your favourite paper. Oo 'as more than a passin' interest in what you and your friends are up to, in order to boost the circulation of 'is quality rag'."

"Newspaper," translated Lexy for Sid.

"How the hell did you manage that?" asked Tom, with a mix of shock and genuine admiration.

"Psychic powers and mathematical deduction," replied Ricky. "And then I just checked out 'er sunscreen pattern on 'er posh phone screen, which she cleans only intermittently. And she's not exactly aware yet, neither."

"So, what happens next?"

"Well I guess we just forward the messages back and forth between the lovely Cheryl and 'er newspaper editor. And then see what 'appens."

"So you've switched his number to yours in her phone memory. Bloody brilliant!" Tom exclaimed.

"Yep. I'm a genius. And then blocked 'is number to 'er. Only just bleedin' managed it in time though. Froze me bollocks off in the pool just after. The fings I do for you…" His sentence hung in the air. "Now for some fun."

"What does *WTFRU* mean?" asked Sid politely.

"I think he's politely enquiring as to her whereabouts," said Lexy.

"Oh! Oh dear… Of course," Sid looked embarrassed for a moment. "I'm not much good at text speak."

"Well there had to be something you're not good at," muttered Dave.

Lexy looked reassuringly at him and squeezed his hand. She winked at him.

"I'm not much good at textin'," said Ricky. "Would you mind?" He handed Lexy his phone.

"You need to see how quickly each one responds," said Lexy. "And hope they don't try to phone each other just yet!"

A reply was coming in from Silky lady.

ON TO IT. CHECKING OUT HOTELS AND LEADS. KNOW WHERE THEY ARE STAYING. BE PATIENT YOB X!

"I think that may mean, you old bastard," added Lexy helpfully. The message was forwarded quickly.

"Why does he think it's coming from her phone?" asked Sid.

"I doubt he knows her number off by heart anyway," said Lexy, "but the international code may be masking her number. We'll make some excuse anyway if we need to. And then at the right moment, we start modifying the messages a little…"

Tom beamed the widest of grins back at her.

*

Back at the five-star hotel, an immaculately dressed waiter was speaking quietly to its newest guest, who was now drinking black coffee in between delicate intakes of blue/grey smoke. She nodded and handed him a folded up note. He gave a little bow and walked back into the hotel. She returned to her phone screen. There seemed to be some lag here in receiving messages in Tenerife. "Roll on Brexit" she muttered to herself. "They can't even get the bloody phones right!"

*

Meanwhile, a man with a bowtie in central London was becoming increasingly irritated in his office. He had temporarily mislaid his phone and was anxious to read his messages. Eventually, his secretary had found it under a newspaper in his room. He muttered a brusque attempt at a "Thank you". He was clearly unpractised in the art. Eventually, a reply was received. He looked at his phone. "About bloody time," he said.

Then he read the message. And then he read it again, but this time more slowly. He grinned to himself. "Got you, you bastards," he said to himself. It came from Myles.

He then forwarded the message to another number in his phone, which was simply noted as 'D' with an accompanying comment.

Its recipient replied *NOTED*. Nothing else.

Ungrateful bastard, thought its sender.

Got the bastard, thought its recipient.

*

Meanwhile, Myles had almost fully recovered from his escapades after arriving on the island. Ann and Rhiannon had made an enormous fuss of him and were genuinely beginning to like him. Despite his timidity, something braver lay somewhere deeper beneath the surface. They had promised to take him back to the cocktail bar once their long daytime shifts had finished, and he had spent much of the afternoon either relaxing or tapping into the hotel's internet.

Later, he had done some shopping and bought himself

some casual canvas trousers, a blue flannel jacket and most importantly, a broad brimmed hat. Finally, he bought himself a new pair of canvas shoes and some aftershave. Along with a little more after-sun cream. As an afterthought, he purchased some sunglasses with proper Polaroid lenses.

"I'm still not sure I trust him," had said Tom.

Lexy had reassured him, and Sid had backed her up without hesitation.

"I trust my instinct," she had said again.

What she didn't know was that Myles had been performing a large financial transaction on behalf of his boss back in London that afternoon. He had also posted a heavy parcel back to London, wrapped in a distinctive carrier bag.

The Crash Team had asked him to keep a low profile in case Cheryl spotted them together, and he had followed their request meticulously.

*

The evening approached and Ricky guided them to their chosen table. This was relatively easy as there weren't any other guests. Rhiannon looked around the bar somewhat aghast. Her day had been exhausting, and she was relieved that the nights were drawing in earlier nowadays, as the pool also closed earlier. She had her white jeans on and was hesitant to plant her own seat on one of these. The light provided by the few remaining naked bulbs was dim to say the least. Dave gallantly wiped one down with a napkin and then placed another on its surface.

Their host looked delighted. "Ladies and gentlemen. The bar is open. And it is happy hour for another fifty-nine minutes. How may I delight your gustatory senses? A cocktail or a beer. Or both?" He added optimistically.

Des had put on his cleanest apron for the occasion and

had even attempted a shave. His creased, weathered old face and seen so much over the years, and furrows which hadn't twitched in months, finally showed signs of movement.

"I could sing for you?" he added.

"Maybe later," replied Tom. "But thank you."

A round was ordered, including two non-alcoholic mocktails, and the conversation began.

At another table, a new guest sat down quietly. She was dressed in unremarkable dark clothes, carried a cheap looking large handbag and showed no signs of interest in any of them. Their conversation continued. Only Ricky noticed the distinctive smell of her cigarettes. And he was already hidden behind a bush in the darkest part of the terrace. Des couldn't believe his luck, another guest! And this one wanted a double vodka tonic too! She would of course get two at this time of day.

*

Back in London, the minister for health was considering his response to his latest message. To his surprise, Gerald from the RMC was asking him to bring forward the announcement by hours. He awaited the return of a package from Tenerife which Myles had organised for him that afternoon.

"My man Myles assures me there is everything in that package to resolve our situation completely," he had added.

The minister considered the request further for a moment and decided to acquiesce. He wanted to end his career at health on a high before developing his ultimate career move. Besides, this could make him some serious money too. Always a bonus. He sent a message to another number. *ANNOUNCEMENT DUE THURS. BUY £100K IN 5S.* He smiled to himself. It was time to open that bottle he kept aside for just this kind of occasion.

*

Back at the bar, they were just starting to enjoy themselves. "Sid, have you brought the bag?" asked Lexy.

"Sid looked worried. No my darling, I couldn't see it in the room, I thought you had it…"

Lexy stood up very suddenly. Her face barely visible in the shadows. She sounded panic stricken. "Oh my God," she said. "Where's the bag?"

Tom looked at her in anguish. "Not the…"

"Yes," she said. "I left it in the room when Myles…" her voice trailed forlornly. And with that she ran from the bar with Sid trailing anxiously in her wake. Tom's famous temper took over now. Furloughed for nearly two days.

Des came across quickly. "Is everything alright?" He looked flustered. "More drinks anyone? Can I assist? Don't go," he begged. "It's still happy…"

Two of his guests had left already and a third was quietly packing her notebook into her oversized bag. She left a five euro note on the table and slipped quietly away from the mayhem. She felt around for her cigarettes but seemed to have misplaced them in the dark.

Meanwhile in a bar a few hundred yards away, a dapper looking man with a less pink forehead was just ordering a cocktail from the waiter in his carefully rehearsed Spanish. He was feeling very pleased with himself indeed. By his side was his new bag containing his other recent purchases and his passport just in case he had to leave in a hurry. The waiter smiled back at him.

"Maybe no ice this time, eh?!"

CHAPTER TWENTY-FIVE: THE AFTERSHOCK

The events that followed had all happened very quickly. A previously unknown minor medical tech company had briefly but spectacularly skyrocketed in price from around fourteen pence a share before peaking at just under fifteen pounds and then crashing even more spectacularly to less than a penny, when the ruse had been discovered.

The RMC chief had been unceremoniously sacked without any explanation after his computer records had been checked, and a new lay member with both vision and morals, had replaced him. His secret bank account had also been mysteriously emptied.

Meanwhile, the minister for health had been moved to 'transport' and a magazine sold in aid of the homeless had made the scoop of the century, after receiving a carefully bound package from the Canary Islands. The national papers had quickly followed with the story. With one notable exception…

*

Some months later, at a large table near the bar, sat eleven friends and an elderly woman who coughed spasmodically, amidst peals of raucous East End laughter. Sid held Lexy's hand. Rhiannon, Dave's. Diego, Ann's. Ricky was telling one of his jokes and although Tom didn't hear most of it, he beamed.

His friend had never looked happier or healthier. He was hosting one of his infamous 'Big Quiz' nights later with his friends from the bar at the nearby hotel, followed by 'Des O'Crooner'. Des always pulled a good crowd now he no longer had the worry of owning and running the place. Turns out, he had a blinder of a voice too. A reply from 'Silky Lady' sat unread in his phone's inbox, although this time it was meant for him. He'd reply later. It was too suggestive to read at the table....

"A toast to our favourite new bar and hotel. El Ricky's!" announced Dave. He patted Rhiannon's enlarging bump affectionately. "And of course to our benefactor and his new husband!" They all cheered, whilst Myles looked delighted and kissed his partner enthusiastically on both cheeks. "Mind the ice, Myles!" They all shouted in unison.

He had timed the peak of the share price rise perfectly with the subsequent press release at the covert privatisation plans. These, of course, had now been put on indefinite hold, much to the annoyance of the PM. Emptying his old boss's secret account had given him the most joy, and then transferring the three and a half million pounds of profit into his own. His parents had even come to the wedding. What was left after the hotel purchase had been anonymously gifted to a homeless ex-serviceman's retreat in North Yorkshire and the NSPCC.

Lexy sent a photo message to her other friend back in London, now promoted from RMC secretary to senior administrator, and soon to join them all for a week's holiday. It seems the temporary number switch trick had worked on her old boss's phone too. He still had absolutely no idea what had happened. Why would he? She had only been his secretary.

"And I still can't believe you didn't tell me," said Sid again to Lexy. "I was so convinced."

"I'm sorry, it had to look genuine," she laughed. "And you trusted me as always. It's a good job it was dark though, I couldn't keep my face straight!"

"We shouldn't keep secrets," Sid replied.

"You mean like your 'worthless' coin collection?! I thought those sovereigns were pound coins! All four hundred of them!"

"Four hundred and two," corrected Sid softly.

"It's a good job I didn't put them in a parking meter by accident, I'd have never realised They look so anonymous."

"It will buy us a small apartment hopefully," smiled Sid in return, squeezing her hand gently.

Tom looked across at the happy scene and smiled. It had all turned out rather well in the end. His daughter was now in regular contact with him again, as was Sid's son, and he had started a small clinic looking after the ex-pats who had fallen on harder times with their own health. He had even set up an alcohol support group for those for whom 'happy hour' was coming a little too frequently. He finally felt both wanted and needed. Even Sid's ex-wife had found romance with a Polish pilot who had taken pity on her after a long flight to Gdansk, as one of the only passengers. She'd finally given up trying to track his phone too. She had all his money anyway.

Meanwhile, a pretty girl in a well-worn but perfectly fitting t-shirt, came to sit on Tom's knee and kissed him gently on the lips. The 'cool and crazy' logo had almost completely worn away from the front now, but the ghostly silhouette of a cool wolf wearing shades on a skateboard still grinned out from it.

"I've been finishing my novel," the ex-librarian said. "It's about us all. I've finally found something interesting to write about. It's amazing what you can find in between the pages of a good book. Lexy co-wrote it with me, and we're calling it *The Crash Team*. Anonymous author, though! What do you think?"

"Bollocks!"

A shrill voice came from a perch in the corner of the bar before Tom could answer Suzie.

Sweep wagged his tail.

GLOSSARY

Crem Form - A Cremation Form. Documentation completed by two independent doctors to confirm that: the death was natural, the body has been carefully examined, the body is free of potentially explosive implanted devices and requires no further investigation. A fee is payable to both doctors, known colloquially as "Ash Cash".

Priapism - A condition causing painful prolonged erection of the penis, sometimes lasting for many hours, and occasionally requiring surgical intervention.

ODP - Operating Department Practitioner; a highly skilled operative assistant.

MI - Myocardial Infarction, known more commonly as a heart attack.

Pontypandy - Fictional town in the popular children's series 'Fireman Sam'.

Larry Hagman - From the fictional character in the TV show 'Dallas', and a slang term for a laryngoscope (a medical torch) used to help insert a breathing tube into the correct place.

ODA - Operating Department Assistant. An alternative title to an ODP

VF - Ventricular Fibrillation. Fatal if untreated. A pulseless heartbeat irregularity - treatable by electric shocks.

CCG - Clinical Commissioning Group, an organisation which commissions most of the hospital and community services in a geographical area.

Long-Term Locum - A temporary doctor who fills in when a regular doctor is away or unavailable.

DTs - Delirium Tremens. The symptoms of withdrawal, usually from long-term alcohol misuse, which can include involuntary shaking, confusion and even death.

Diawl Budur - Welsh for dirty devil!

FBC and **U&Es** - These are commonly requested blood tests. A Full Blood Count and Urea and Electrolytes.

Jack Duckworth - A character from the ITV series 'Coronation Street', famed for often wearing badly self-repaired glasses.

SHO - Senior House Officer. The first grade of junior doctor after completing the initial registration year after qualifying.

Apgar Score - A scoring system to assess the vital signs of a new-born baby, usually checked at 1 and 5 minutes of age.

Scooby Doo - A nickname for SCBU or Special Care Baby Unit.

Printed in Great Britain
by Amazon